Road to Two Hearts

Theron J. Parker

and

Patricia A. Heggs

PublishAmerica
Baltimore

First printing

ISBN: 1-4241-3146-4
PUBLISHED BY PUBLISHAMERICA, LLLP
www.publishamerica.com
Baltimore

Printed in the United States of America

ROAD TO TWO HEARTS

Happiness Always
Theron J Parker

Theron J. Parker 7-07-07

and

Patricia A. Heggs

Thank you for your support
Patricia A. Heggs
7/7/07

Dedication

To my father, Theron F. Parker, thanks for believing that I had the potential to shoot for the stars

-Theron

My Uncle Bernard Parker and my Aunt Joyce Parker, thanks for being there when I was a teenager. Your gift of love helped me reached my goals

-Theron

To my mother, Ruby Sims, thanks for your love and the gift of wisdom

-Patricia

Acknowledgements

Wife and kids: Sandy Parker, Marcus, Manguell, Theron Jr., Jessica Davis, James, and Joshua Parker

Mother: Catherine Parker

My Sisters: Brenda Lockett, Gwendolyn Sanders, Dorine Stephenson and Denise Parker

My Brothers: Ricky Parker, Kevin Parker and Phillip Parker.

Husband: Joseph Heggs, the love of my life

My Sisters: Virginia Mays and LaVern Lundy

My Daughter: Tuvache Moody

My Nieces: Rae' Lundy, and Monica Greenwood

My Nephew Arthur Rocker

-Patricia

Also By Theron J. Parker

Poetry:

Poems from the Heart
Visions of True Love

INTRODUCTION

No one really knows why events in life occurs the way they do. People have asked this question since the dawn of time. These events cause us to look back at our lives, always wondering why we have had failures and successes. Ann Taylor and Douglas Brown were born in the heart of the south. I mean right smack in the middle. The license plate on all cars championed the slogan "The Peach State."

Ann Taylor had made up her mind that nothing would stop her from getting her education and achieving whatever goals she set for herself. Even though she has had bad luck with men, she never gave up on finding Mr. Right. She guessed it was finally her turn to receive a little happiness.

Douglas Brown was a retired military serviceman. He had met Ms. Right each time he got married; however, he could never make his marriage work or last the duration. For some odd reason, being happily married was like a bad hair cut...**It just didn't work.** Douglas had made up his mind that he was not going to get seriously involved anymore. He was only going to date and admire the beauty of women. I guess in some odd way, their new encounters were both Ann and Douglas's "little piece of happiness."

~ Chapter One ~

Ann Going Home

I can see it clearly in my mind as if it were yesterday. The police sergeant was knocking on the bathroom door asking me if I was okay. I can still feel the sting from the force of Spencer's hand across my face. Tears fell from my eyes like a rainforest monsoon. There was a big hole in the bathroom door where he had discharged the old 12-gauge shotgun. The only reason I was still alive is because I hid in the cast iron bathtub we had purchased from a flea market the year before. I guess the second reason is because the shotgun jammed the second time Spencer tried to shoot it.

Spencer had completely flipped out this time. The constant drinking and marijuana smoking had made him lose his reality. Nothing has been the same after his stroke. He had become jealous and suspicious about everything. Spencer was a bitter man. He accused me of infidelity with every man that looked in my direction. I would get embarrassed because he would chase men away who only smiled politely at me.

Shortly after Spencer attacked me, the police arrived. One of the policemen asked me to get out of the tub and open the door. I could see Spencer lying on the floor handcuffed. His eyes had the look of a rabid dog. The police kept telling him to be still and not to move. He was spitting, still trying to get at me.

As I left the bathroom, I was escorted to the living room where the sergeant in charge consoled me as I attempted to regain my composure. The sergeant asked me if I needed to go to the hospital. I said no. He strongly recommended that I spend the night with a family member. It would have been nice; however, I didn't have any family living in Prattville.

Shortly afterward, Spencer's brother-in-law arrived. Sam was the chief of police in Prattville, a small rural town in Ohio.

"Are you ok Ann?"

"No, I am not Sam. Spencer just tried to kill me."

"I heard the call on the radio. I got here as fast I could."

"Thanks sergeant," I said, as Spencer was being lead out the door to the awaiting squad car.

Sam sat beside me putting his arms around my shoulders. I completely loss my composure and cried uncontrollably.

"What do you need me to do Ann?"

"I need to call my sister in Georgia. I have to leave here!"

"Yes, I understand. Are you going to press charges? If you don't, we can only hold Spencer seventy-two hours."

"I don't know what I am going to do Sam. I do know for a fact that I need to leave here."

"Who do you want me to call?"

"I need to call my sister, let me get my address book."

I walked slowly to the nightstand in my bedroom to retrieve my address book.

"Here is Lisa's number Sam. Can you dial it for me?"

Sam dialed the number and handed me the phone.

"Here you go Ann."

"Thanks."

"Hello, Lisa!"

"Yes."

"This is Ann." I sobbed.

"Girl, why are you crying?"

"Spencer totally lost it. He tried to kill me!"

"What?"

"Yes he tried to shoot me. The police just took him away. I am here with Sam."

"Girl, get your clothes together and catch a plane tonight and fly back to Atlanta. We will figure it all out after you have had some time to calm down."

"Lisa, can you make me a plane reservation for tomorrow morning; I am too shaken up right now to coordinate anything."

"Yes, I can. Let me speak to Sam."

"Here is Sam."

"What in the hell is wrong with Spencer?" Asked Lisa?

"I don't know. I am just as surprised as anyone. Ann has been the pillar of support for Spencer since his stroke. She has cared for him like any good woman would. I guess he must have been drinking while on his medication. The doctor warned him about what could happen if he drinks alcohol while the medication is in his system. He was totally out of it when I arrived. My deputies had to restrain him. I told the sergeant to take him to lockup at the mental ward. We will hold him for a minimum of seventy-two hours."

"Seventy-two hours! You need to keep him locked up forever. What is wrong with him trying to kill Ann? I knew she should not have married him."

"I understand how you feel Lisa; however, you know his family is highly respected in these parts and his father will probably have him out on bail as soon as he can. I will help Ann get her things together and catch a flight out when you schedule it."

"Okay Sam, I'll call Ann back as soon as I arrange her flight."

Sam put the receiver on the hook.

"Did she hang up?"

"Yes, she did," said Sam.

"Ann, please explain what happened."

I told Sam I didn't really know what caused Spencer to go off the deep end. When I returned home Spencer was standing in the hallway looking angry. He has been acting really strange over the last two months. I had noticed a slight change in behavior but I didn't pay much attention to it. I was always mindful of what the doctor had told Spencer. He knew he couldn't have anything to drink while the medication was in his system. Spencer must have been drinking.

While I was cooking supper, Spencer grabbed me by the hair and threw me to the floor. He began to hit me and yell that I was with some other man. I had only come home a few minutes late because I stopped at the grocery store to pick up some fresh collard greens and tomatoes. I really don't understand why he went off today. I had planned on cooking him an old fashioned southern supper. I have tried my best to be attentive to him. I know the stroke has affected the part of his brain that deals with reality and the medication he takes helps him stay focused on the present while treating his anxiety and depression. I have tried hard not to have anything that contained alcohol in the house because I feared something like this would happen.

Last month while I was cleaning up in the basement, I found a telephone-recording device under the stairs. I was shocked to find out that he had been recording my telephone conversations. I never said anything to him because I didn't have anything to hide. I hoped he would listen to the tapes and see that I was not talking to any other man. I made every attempt to strengthen our relationship. No matter what I did to make things better for us, his jealousy and suspicion got worst.

"Excuse me Ann, you were talking about tonight."

"I am sorry Sam, like I said he just hit me repeatedly. I ran upstairs and locked the bathroom door. Spencer kept kicking it and cursing at me. He had gone mad. I still don't know what triggered it. I jumped in the tub. I thought he would break the door down and start hitting me again. Shortly afterward, Spencer stopped kicking the door and shouting for a minute and then I heard the gun go off. It blew a hole in the door near the doorknob. I thought I was dead. I passed out. When I came to, I heard the policeman calling to me through the hole in the door. I guess one of the neighbors must have called the police. I just lay there, scared out of my wits until the police asked me if I was ok and for me to unlock the door. So you see, it all happened so quickly. I believe the medication caused him to be jealous and paranoid while I was out shopping. Sam, you know how good I have been to him. Spencer changed so much since the day he had the stroke."

"Yes, I know Ann. I had discussed Spencer's problem with his sister. She has talked to him on several occasions trying to reassure him that you loved him."

The phone rang.

"Hello, this is Ann."

"Are you ok," asked my mother.

"Yes mother. Sam is here with me and the police took Spencer to lockup at the mental ward."

"Ann, I am here with Lisa. She has you scheduled to fly out on Delta flight 319 at 12:00 p.m. to Atlanta. You need to get your things together and be ready to go. Is there someone who can take you to the airport?"

"Yes mother, Sam said he will come by in the morning and take me."

"Make sure you take everything you can carry and all the money you can withdraw from your account."

"I will mother and don't worry I'm safe now. I will be all right tonight. Spencer will not be able to get out of lockup for at least seventy-two hours. Tell Lisa I said thanks. I will call you in the morning before I leave to go to the airport. Good night, Mom."

"Okay, baby. If you need anything don't hesitate to call me and let me know."

"Okay mother I will. Good night."

My mother hung up the phone and I stood there wishing I were at home in Georgia with her.

"Well, its getting late Ann. Is there anything else I can do before I leave?"

"No, Sam thanks for everything."

"I will see you in the morning."

Sam checked the door one last time before he said good night and locked the door behind him.

I tried to calm down and go to sleep. I couldn't. I kept hearing Spencer screaming at me over and over. I felt as though I was still in the bathtub laying in the fetal position. The thoughts were too much for me to bear. I laid in bed and tried again to sleep. After a few hours, I finally found the strength to close my eyes and sleep.

During the night, I dreamed of how wonderful Spencer was when I first met him. I thought about the night he proposed to me when we lived in Atlanta. Everything was great then. It all turned bad the weeks following his stroke. He became a different person. I did all I could to help him adjust. It all came to this one night of complete horror.

When morning came I was still tired from the night's ordeal. I took a shower in the guest bathroom. I looked at the bruise left on my face by Spencer's hand. My cheeks were slightly swollen. I put on my make-up, got dressed and packed everything I could carry on the plane with me. I knew in my mind I would never return to live with Spencer, because I couldn't give Spencer another chance to kill me. The medication and his inability to stop drinking would eventually become too unpredictable. I could one day find myself dead or lying in a hospital room trying to recover from his abuse. I cared for Spencer, but he could not control his anger or his suspicions any more. He had become too paranoid about everything.

Outside, I could hear Sam's car pulling into the driveway. I rolled my suitcases to the front door. Sam was standing there. He said good morning as he took the suitcases from me and loaded them in his trunk. I stood there looking out over the front yard on what had seemed before as the perfect place to spend the rest of my life. I had so many good memories and now in one terrible night all was lost. The man I was willing to spend the rest of my life with tried to kill me. The man for whom I left Georgia to make a better life with was now locked up in jail.

Sam and I drove down the dusty road not saying much to each other. We just looked straight ahead. He knew I really loved Spencer, but the events that happened the night before was too much for any normal person to take. When we arrived at the airport, Sam got out and opened my door. I just sat there still traumatized.

"Ann, are you getting out?"

"Yes Sam, I'm sorry. Thanks for everything. Tell everyone I said good-by."

"They will understand Ann and if they don't, the hell with them. You need to get back to Georgia where you can be with your family."

"Yes, you are right."

Sam gave my luggage to the attendant. I gave him a big hug and thanked him for his kindness. He looked at me as though he could feel my sadness. As he was getting in the car, I told him I would not be pressing charges against Spencer. I was leaving and that was good enough.

Before going to the terminal, I stopped by the bank and got a cashier's check for every dime that was in Spencer and my joint account. I would need it to start my new life. There was no way I could ever go back to Spencer. I was too afraid of him now. I would always be thinking he would be standing there with the shotgun ready to blow my head off. I wanted to go home to Georgia and lay my head in my mother's lap. I needed the comfort of my family. I needed them to be around me.

During the flight to Atlanta, I couldn't help but wonder why this happened to me. I thought I had finally met the man of my dreams. We had a beautiful house and the two of us had great jobs. We had a great retirement plan. It seemed as though we would be happy forever. I loved Spencer so much. I did all I could to help him recover from his stroke. I guess I was destined to go through one more challenge.

When I arrived at the airport in Atlanta, my mother and two sisters were standing at the gate ready to burst through and hug me. Tears started to roll down my face. I dropped everything that I was carrying and fell in their collective arms.

"Everything is all right now child. Don't you be afraid? You are here with your family now. We will work things out."

Lisa and Mary both were crying with me. I collected my belongings and we proceeded to the checkout. My stepfather was waiting outside in the car as we brought the luggage to the curve. He loaded everything in the trunk of his car and we drove away. All of this was like a bad dream.

"Tell me what happened," asked Mary.

"I really don't want to talk about it right now. It was the most terrible thing that can happen after you had given your all and the person you love snaps on you and tries to take your life."

"He tried to kill you for real?", asked Mary.

"Yes, he did. I knew Spencer was becoming unstable. I just didn't know how much. Through all of his accusations and threats, I tried to reaffirm that I was faithful. Spencer could not believe I only wanted him. He kept telling me that the breakups of my previous marriages were my fault. He had become a mad man. No matter what I did he was always checking up on me. He even put a tape recorder in the basement to record all calls that came in or out. I didn't say anything because I had nothing to hide. I was just hoping he would get better.

"Leave her be. Ann has been through enough for one day."

"Okay mother," said Lisa and Mary. I laid my head in my mother's lap and slept during the thirty-five mile drive from the airport.

When we arrived at my mother's house, everyone was there to welcome me home. My daughter and son-in-law had driven up from Miami, Florida. I had not called her because I didn't want her to worry. I knew my mother would contact her. She ran to me with tears in her eyes asking if I was ok. All of the people I loved were there when I needed them the most. We all went into the house where my mother cooked us lunch and I told them the entire story from start to finish.

Tonight I don't have to worry about Spencer or what I am going to do with the rest of my life. I am safe living with my sister outside of Atlanta, Georgia. My world may have gotten smaller, but my mind is clearer. I know I will have to start divorce proceedings in the months ahead, but tonight I will lay in the comfort of my sister's bed. I will say my prayers and thank God for a kind, loving family. I was ready to go to sleep when Lisa knocked on the door.

"Are you sleep?" asked Lisa.

"No, not really," I said with one eye almost closed. Lisa sat down next to me and started to rub my back.

"It's ok Ann, I understand how you feel. Remember when I lived in New York for two years? I had a friend named Joan who was married to this guy named Carl. He was a very nice person. Carl was well known in the community. He volunteered at his church and at the local Boys Club. No one ever thought that he would be a violent man.

My friend Joan had spent the day cleaning her house and preparing Carl a great supper. That particular evening, she was wearing his favorite black nightgown. Carl had stopped at the neighborhood bar to have a drink with a few of his buddies before going home. Some college students from NYU were celebrating passing their final exams. Carl didn't drink much. He stopped by the bar just to be sociable. Carl had gotten up to go to the men's room. While passing the bar, he ordered a Long Island Iced Tea. The college students were pretty wild. One of the students accidentally bumped into Carl. Thinking nothing of it, Carl said excuse me and continued to walk toward the men's room.

A couple of the college students got angry and pushed Carl against the wall. Carl almost fell on the floor. The students looked very angrily at him while he collected himself and went into the men's room. Carl decided to let the incident pass. However before Carl came out, one of the college students not involved in the incident told the bartender that he was going to buy the man that went into the men's room a drink. The bartender told him that he had fixed him a Long Island Iced Tea and that it was sitting on the counter. As a token of good will, the student paid for it. While the bartender was putting the money into the cash machine, another student that was involved in the incident had a similar thought in mind; however, he did not intend to be nice to Carl. He took the drink from the counter and dropped acid into it.

Carl's friends had seen the altercation but thought it was no big deal. When Carl returned to the bar, the bartender told him that the drink was on the college student. Carl raised his drink to him in a jester of good will. Carl had no clue what the other student had done. It was discovered when they went to trial."

"What trial?" I asked.

"Carl was on trial for attempted murder."

"Attempted murder!"

"Yes, when Carl went home the acid had mixed with Carl's blood pressure medication and caused him to hallucinate. He thought his wife Joan was a burglar that broke into the house. He shot her five times. He had no clue as to who she was. The police arrested Carl for attempted murder. It was a miracle that Joan survived. Carl had totally flipped out. At his trial, the college student that purchased the drink for Carl told the entire unfortunate story. Joan somehow fully recovered. Carl never did. He is in a mental institution in up state New York. So you see I understand how lucky you are."

"Thanks Lisa. I understand what you are trying to say. Good night, I need to rest."

"Good night Ann."

~ Chapter Two ~

Douglas Brown

I've had my fair share of failed relationships. I was in my first marriage and I knew it would not last long. I guess you can say the writing was on the wall. I married an Asian girl that I had hoped would be the cure all for my life. She was one of the prettiest Asian women that God had put on the face of the earth. But all her beauty could not hide the volatile personality that lived deep within her. Her name was Mi Yong. I met her during an assignment oversees while stationed in Manheim, Germany. I didn't know it at the time, but Germany has a large oriental population.

I was at a club doing what I enjoy doing the most. Yes, dancing I was disco dancing my butt off. Even though it was the mid eighties, disco was alive and well in Germany. However, if I knew then what I know now, I would have left her on the dance floor where I first said hello.

Things started off great at first. I was the king and she was the answer to all my needs. I tried to give her all the things she asked for. She wanted her citizenship, her GED, and her college degree. She wanted her parents to come and live with us. There was nothing she could ask that I could not deliver. Life as we knew it was great. At least I thought so, but what I didn't know is that down deep inside Mi Yong was a volcano ready to explode. It had been lying inactive during the first three years of our marriage. Yes, old Mount Mi Yong was getting ready to explode.

You know, most scientists have an earthquake meter of some kind that tells them that a volcanic eruption may take place. The only thing I had was the occasional, "well, we haven't had an argument for a long time" speech. I should have been smart enough to detect that something terrible was going to happen down the road. Let me see, I believe the eruption was apparent when she asked me, "Have you seen the Saudi Airline vouchers?"

"Yes, I tore them up."

"You tore them up!"

"Yes, I did MiYong."

"Why did you tear them up? You are a crazy black man."

"Well, the last time we got into an argument I told you that we were not going on any more trips and we needed to save our money so we can return to the states debt free."

Now, I know the term debt free is not what most women understand. However, I wanted Mi Yong to know that it was a real goal of mine.

"All you men are just alike, always running through life with shit for brains."

"Mi Yong!" I said loudly. Why is it that every time we get on the road to debt recovery you want to go the other direction?"

"Because all men have shit for brains," she said in a loud voice.

Mi Yong ran up stairs and started to yell at her parents in Korean. Well, I never learned how to speak Korean and didn't want to start now. Suddenly, her father ran down stairs shaking his head. He was saying something in a low voice as he passed me pausing only to give me a ritual bow, as it was his custom. I nodded my head in return and headed upstairs to finish the conversation MiYong had started that was a bad idea. Her mother and she were locked in a fierce conversation. I withdrew and proceeded to go and enjoy doing what I like to do best. Yes you know it, plant my big butt right in front of the television. Instead of setting on my ass, I should have looked in my crystal ball to see what life had in store for me.

Months later, I was assigned the distinguished duty of escorting several Saudi Nationals to the United States. While we were there, they would tour several civilian and military communications facilities. The Saudis were really impressed with the tour they received. The American tour sponsor really laid out the red carpet and put forth their best effort. I had heard that on their prior trips, the touring company had really fallen on their face. It had taken several years for them to get back into the favor of the Saudis. After two weeks of facility touring in the United States, we would depart and go to France where we would visit the French civilian and military communications facility. It was indeed a great trip for all involved. I had never in my life been treated like a welcome dignitary in every place I visited. I was a king for a month.

We arrived in the states landing at the Kennedy International Airport in Queens, New York. We had connecting flights to Boston at LaGuardia Airport. I didn't know how mischievous my Saudi counterparts could be. The ride to LaGuardia Airport was the most frightening trip I had ever taken in a taxi. As we began to drive, each of my Saudi buddies would take turns teasing the taxi driver about being a New Yorker and how timid they are while driving a taxi. One would brag about how taxis drivers in Saudi were fearless and could drive in and out of the most difficult traffic. The other would taut the taxi driver on his taxi driving incompetence. It was as if they both had a death wish. This playfulness agitated the taxi driver to no end. To prove his point, the taxi driver would dart in and out of heavy traffic on the Brooklyn Queens Expressway. The French officer and I thought seriously about exiting the vehicle the next time it stopped. When we finally arrived at the airport, I had two stiff shots of Hennessey to help recover from the taxi ordeal. I was elated to be out of the taxis and sitting in a chair awaiting our connecting flight. There are some things in life that you rather not experience; riding in a New York taxi while someone is pissing off the driver is one of them.

Our trip in the states took two weeks. The touring company escorted us everywhere. It was an opportunity of a lifetime for me. I had never in my entire life been treated with respect due an officer of my rank. I could have remained on the assignment forever. Like all good things, the tour came to an end. We soon concluded our tour of the communications facilities in the states and departed to France.

While in France, I had the opportunity to visit Paris and the city for which New Orleans was named, Orlean. All of the cities had history that you would not believe. It was great. I walked every street I possibly could. The only thing I was missing was the lady in my life. Well, I was still in love but I think my wife, Mi Yong had other things in mind.

As our French tour was coming to a close, I called my house to let the volcano know I would be returning soon. The phone rang and rang. No one ever picked up the phone. I made several calls that night and the following morning. I finally gave up and called a buddy of mine that was scheduled to pick me up at the airport.

"What's up?" replied J.R.

"I am due to come home in four days."

"Man if I was you, I would come home now."

"What do you mean?"

"Hey, just come home as quick as you can."

Well, it didn't take a rocket scientist to figure out that Mount Mi Yong had gone and made a complete ass out of herself. I briefed my Saudi counterparts and left the next day.

I returned to Saudi Arabia late on a Wednesday night. J.R. picked me up from the airport and informed me that MiYong was over to his house. It seemed strange that he would recommend that I return home and then let my wife stay at his house with his family. He must have thought that I was going to beat her brains out. The whole ordeal was perplexing.

After I arrived at his house, I had a long talk with her and decided it was best that she return to the States. Her parents would also go back and live with her aunt in New Jersey. I didn't want to deal with the issue. I found out after the three of them had left that she had gotten drunk and allowed herself to get involved in a sex party on one of the other American facilities in Saudi. I knew a party was going to be hosted at a sister compound while I was gone on my escort duty in the states. I knew the guy who hosted the party. I also knew that a lot of the American military and civilians would be attending. I had asked Mi Yong not to go because. I knew how vulnerable she became after she had one too many drinks. No one would be there to protect her from herself. This was a big fear of mine.

That night, I departed to drop my car at the military compound, we stopped at the military version of a convenience store to purchase some gum for the fourteen-hour airplane ride I had to take. Like most wives, she forgot something and went back into the store. Little did I know, she went and purchased a rubber. She gave it to me as a joke. However, it would be a sign that signaled the end of our marriage. Even now the details are too painful to tell. It was embarrassing. People who had never attended one of my social functions were coming by the house to pay their respect as if MiYong had died. It was a very trying period in my life. When I look back on it, I can see that it was something I should have seen coming. The volcano had to erupt. It had to spew its lava all over my life. I guess I deserved it for deeds I had committed while moving in and out of previous relationships. Yes, Mount Mi Yong had exploded and scattered my life all over Saudi.

~ Chapter Three ~

Ann's Divorce

Spencer continued to call me after he got out of jail. I just could not go back to him. The experience was too traumatic for me. The love I had for him had died that night. The rage that was in him was like watching a horror movie. I kept seeing a vision of Jack Nicholson trying to push the door open with an ax in his hand. To make matters more aggravating for Spencer, while he was still in jail I flew back to Ohio with my daughter and her husband Darnell. I rented a U-Haul and loaded all of my personal things I had collected over the years and prepared to start the trip back to Atlanta, Georgia. Before I left, I contacted a local attorney I knew from functions I attended while living in Ohio. He did not know Spencer and was willing to take my divorce case. This was the last thing I needed to do. As soon as I closed the loop with the attorney we set out on our way back to Atlanta. My son-in-law drove the U-Haul while my daughter and I rode in the BMW Spencer and I purchased the year before. This was it. All of my things were packed in cardboard boxes inside the U-haul truck.

Several months later after returning to Georgia, I received the official paperwork for the divorce hearing. I was to return to Ohio in October. This would be the first time I would see Spencer since the night he tried to kill me. I was a little afraid to return. My lawyer assured me that he would take precautions to ensure my safety. As the day approached, my sister Lisa had agreed to fly up to Ohio with me and attend the proceeding. It wouldn't take long because a lot of the property disbursement had been agreed upon prior to my arrival.

I felt better having Lisa by my side. She had experienced dealing with men like Spencer. While attending Georgia State University she was stalked by a local guy she had met at Club Ecstasy in downtown Atlanta. They dated several times. She found out that he was using drugs heavily and decided to break it off. He would not accept no for an answer.

One night while she was at the club, he asked her to come outside so they could talk. When she didn't, he slapped her across the face and punched her. He kept calling and showing up on campus. She told him to leave her alone and she never wanted to see him again. He still would not take no for an answer. Even though she got a restraining order he would always show up on campus jumping around corners surprising her. She always had to have someone with her.

Eventually, she had to take matters into her own hands. She went to the local Wal-Mart and purchased a pellet pistol. It had the look of a .38 caliber handgun. She carried it with her all the time on campus. One night after class, she was walking through the archway and noticed he was looking around the corner. She put the pistol in her hand and as soon as he stuck his head around the corner she fired. It scared the guy so that he never bothered her again. Lisa was tough. I needed her toughness with me.

Once we arrived at the airport, my lawyer and a sheriff's deputy were there waiting to escort us to the courtroom. My lawyer thought it was wise to take the extra precaution. When we arrived at the courtroom Spencer, was already there. He looked at me with evilness in his eyes. His entire family had come out to support him. I had only my sister and my lawyer in the courtroom with me for moral support.

"Will the plaintiff and respondent please stand. Do either of you have anything else to add at this time?"

Spencer represented himself. He shook his head answering no.

"No judge." My lawyer and I said no at the same time. Everything was read per our agreement. The judge asked Spencer if he understood. Spencer was so upset he only made grunting noises. It was as if my presence was releasing Spencer's rage all over again.

The judge raised his voice a little louder, "Mr. Maddox do you understand how the court has decreed that assets will be divided?" Spencer just stood there grunting, looking at me and then at the judge. The deputy standing next to me placed his hands on his revolver. Spencer noticed and grunted a yes answer back to the judge. The judge declared that I could assume my maiden name "Taylor" if I wished to do so. I was glad the proceeding and my life in Ohio were finally over. My lawyer told me that he would send the final paper work as soon as it was filed.

As we started to depart the courtroom, Spencer made a mad dash toward Lisa and me. Sam had assigned a deputy to sit back and observe every move Spencer made. When Spencer reached for me, the deputy grabbed him and tossed him to the floor. Sam held Spencer while the deputy handcuffed him. He had flipped out again. Spencer was on the floor foaming at the mouth, he couldn't speak. He just kept making grunting sounds like when the judge asked him a question.

His family members tried to comfort him, but Sam told them to stay back. Sam had to perform his official duty and place Spencer under arrest for attempted assault. He knew Spencer had lost control and needed medical help. I felt sorry for Spencer but I feared for my life more. Lisa and I left the building headed straight for the airport.

On the flight home, I wondered how this man I had given my heart to could hate me so much. I had sold my house in Atlanta, gave up my job, and moved to Ohio to be with him. He was supposed to be the one and only man I would spend the rest of my life with.

However, that would be the last time I saw Spencer. He never called or came back to Atlanta again. My lawyer sent me a check for my portion of the settlement less his fee. I was happy and was ready to start my life over. The check was made out in my maiden name, Ann Taylor.

Before leaving Atlanta to attend my divorce proceeding in Ohio, I had scheduled a job interview with BellSouth located in downtown Atlanta. I was interviewing for an office manager's position in charge of accounts receivable. I was excited about my return trip to Atlanta and the possibility of a new job.

The next day, I prepared for my job interview. I was as clean as they come. No one would ever guess that I had just been through hell in a hand basket. I was scheduled to interview with Mr. Green, the southeastern district manager. I was told a lot of nice things about him when I had visited the office to get a job application and do a little homework. I was even fortunate enough to meet him coming in the office the day I was there. Sheila Brown, the receptionist had also given me the 411 on him. Looking back on that day, I believe Mr. Green liked me right from the start.

My trip to downtown Atlanta was slow. Traffic and more traffic was everywhere. As I made it to the office location, I was exhausted from the heat. I made a quick dash to the ladies room before reporting for my interview. After freshening up, I was ready to answer any question that came my way. As I left the ladies room, I met Sheila Brown, the office receptionist.

"Good Morning. How are you today?"

"Good Morning Sheila. It is nice seeing you again."

"Oh, you remembered my name."

"Yes I did. If I am going to be working here, I better start remembering people's names right away," I said smiling.

"Well, okay Ms. Taylor. Please have a seat in the reception area and Mr. Green will come and escort you to the conference room in a minute."

Sheila called Mr. Green to let him know that I had arrived. Like clock work, Mr. Green came out his office.

"Good morning Ann. How are you on this beautiful morning?"

"I am great Mr. Green. I am looking forward to the possibility of working for Bellsouth."

"I am happy to hear that Ann. Before we get started, I would like to introduce you to Cynthia Brannon and Flora Cannon."

"Good morning Ann. Nice to meet you," said the two of them.

Cynthia was the Yellow Pages account manager and Flora managed new accounts.

I took a seat and the questions came. Each of them took turns asking me question after question concerning accounting and office management. I gave correct answers to each of their questions. I could see the three of them looking back and forth at each other with a little smile on their faces. Finally, Mr. Green asked the last question of the interview.

"Ann, I think I can speak for all of us. Can you start working next Monday?"

I was so happy inside I could burst. I contained my excitement and answered, "Yes, I can."

Each of them congratulated me and welcomed me aboard. I couldn't wait to leave the office and call my mother and sisters. I could finally start my life over in Georgia. As I left the office, I was filled with total excitement. I called my mother and told her the great news.

"I got the job Mom!" I am the new manager of account receivables for the southeast district of Bellsouth.

"Congratulations Ann, I told you not to worry."

"I know you did mom. It just has been awhile since I worked full time. I was glad that Mr. Green didn't hold that against me."

"They knew that they had an experienced person that can make a great contribution to their organization."

"You are right as usual mom. I'll call you tomorrow."

"Okay baby, congratulations again!"

~ Chapter Four ~

The Day I Met Ann Taylor

Time has a way of catching up with you. I met Ann Taylor one year ago this pass September. I lost my breath when we were introduced.

"If I can be of help, please let me know," I uttered as my chest filled with air?

I watched her as she walked away. Suddenly, she turned back as if she knew I was watching her. Giving me a warm smile, she faded around the corner.

Returning to my office, I pondered over what had taken place. I knew in my mind that my life was complete. Although, I had made several bad decisions in previous relationships, I knew I was currently on the right track. Smiling to myself, I dismissed the thoughts as a random encounter.

I guess it is only fair to say, Ann was a **browning by Jamaican definition**. She stood five feet six inches tall. She had long black hair and redefined the term "curves." Ann was able to make an old pair of overalls look good. She topped everything off with a pleasant smile and eyes that sparkled. Her demeanor was so pleasing, that co-workers would visit her office just to relax. Ann was a graduate of Georgia State University. She had received her degree in marketing. Her life had taken several uneventful turns, which brought her back to the Atlanta.

As I stated earlier, I did not understand the reason I had become spellbound. It had to be something that was triggered from a prior life. I was happily divorced and had just moved to Atlanta. Everything was looking up. I had been working for Bellsouth for the past five months. We were in the process of moving to a new location in a few weeks. The current office no longer met our needs. The company was expanding.

Everyone in the office enjoyed my vibrant personality. Everyone except for Darla Nelson, she thought I was stuck on myself. She really didn't have a clue that it was all a masquerade. I had to build myself up so everyone would have confidence in my ability to do my job. I figured she did not like me because I was retired from the Air Force and Darla's ex-husband was a retired master sergeant. Several of the co-workers felt that she still harbored bad feelings for anyone that had served in the armed services.

During Ann's orientation, I had the honor of briefing her on the operational aspects of the office. I escorted her to the mailroom where she had just been assigned her new mail cubbyhole. I highlighted the main point of mail distribution and how everything got from point a to z. We then proceeded to the reproduction room where I gave her a briefing on the office layout and all of the services that were provided for all employees. I then took her to my office and made sure she understood that I was there to provide her with the very best in operational support if and when she required my assistance. Last but not least, I gave her a tour of the Technology room. I briefed her on every nook and cranny.

As we prepared to depart, she turned away to point towards a desk and as she faced me, the light shined in her eyes and made them sparkle. For some reason, I became mesmerized and found myself being pulled towards her. It was as if we were negative and positive ends of two magnets. We stood there for several minutes. Something told me to open my eyes before I made a complete ass of myself. Somehow, I did and was able to regain my senses. You know, I have never been the same since that encounter.

I finished my tour of the office with Ann and escorted her back to her desk. While in her office we sat and talked, exchanging trivial conversation. I told her that I had just specialized in business technology since getting out of the Air Force. I further explained that I had been trained as a supply technician. I was responsible for a lot of people and equipment during my distinguished tour of service. I had grown tired of management and wanted to try my hands on the technical side of the road. Ann just sat there smiling, not saying much. Her warmth seems to take all of my troubles away and relax me. Finally, I stopped talking about myself and asked her the big question.

"Are you married?"

She seemed startled. She stated she had just gotten a divorce from her husband. The marriage ended in a mess. The poor man had flipped out and tried to hurt her before her departure from Ohio. She stated it was a long story and she did not want to get into the details. I said I understood. I concluded my conversation by issuing one last welcome and restating my desire to be of assistance. As I walked out of Ann's office, a funny feeling came over me. I thought hard about the incident in the computer room.

Returning to my office, I sat in my chair conducting some self-counseling. I tried to figure out what happened to make me lose my sense of direction. I wondered what magic had been cast that held me spellbound. I had actually tried to kiss Ann on her lips. I was drawn to her like a moth to a flame. I thought to myself, "I hoped she did not realize that I had tried to kiss her." I hoped her back was turned when I leaned forward. I wished all of this was just a dream and none of it really happened. I did not want to revisit any of my prior exploits.

Sure she was interesting, but the "needs of the many outweighed the desires of the one." Mr. Spock from Star Trek said something like that. I soon dismissed the incident and went on my way trying to re-enter the daily activities of the office by providing excellent operational support to the many different personalities.

The next week, Ms. Anderson asked if I could give a road test to Ann and one of the other new female employees. All new employees had to be road tested. I did not mind since I could have been stuck in the office listening to Mattie Crenshaw complain about everything. I scheduled the test drive for the following day. Both of them agreed to drive along the routes where each of them had major clients and facilities.

The next day came soon enough. I gave both of them their safety briefing prior to them starting on their routes. Ms. Sanders was the first to drive. It was a beautiful day and every opportunity I got, I looked back at Ann. Ms. Sanders was pleasant; however, I was just not interested. There are certain people you meet in your lifetime that just have a powerful effect on you. Case in point for me was Ann.

As we continued with the test drive, Ms. Sanders informed us that she had driven bigger vehicles than the sixteen-seat passenger van. She provided a detailed history of her experience. Well, I guess you know, I mentally went to sleep as soon as she said, "when I." There you have it. When I woke up, or should I say when it was Ann's turn to get in the driver's seat, she commanded my full attention. She impressed me from the start. She made sure all of the mirrors were correct. She drove as though she was a pilot preparing to take off on the runway. It was a magical thing to watch. Ann was so relaxed and confident that I let her drive all the way back to the office. Yes, watching her drive was a thing of beauty. As we arrived at the office park, I had spent too much time telling Ann what a great job driving she did. Ms. Sanders was soon on my case, telling me to wipe the dribble off of my lip.

"Excuse me, Douglas," she blurted out.

Ms. Sanders quickly explained that there were two employees that had a road test. I came to my senses and offered an apology to both of them stating what a great job they did on the road test.

As you can see, this was the theme at the office. Never make a fuss about any one female co-worker unless you were prepared to tell all of them that they were great. I knew better, I had just been sidetracked. I should have remembered the right jab I received in my back from Darla Nelson.

Later that evening, I dropped by Jay's Bar and Grill. I stopped by every so often to keep my skills fine tuned. When I arrived, my friend John was already up to no good trying to convince one of the new arrivals that he should be the one she goes with home tonight with. John was a true player. I have to admit, I could learn a thing or two from him.

"Hi John, what's kicking?"

"You are my brother."

"I see you are still trying to get the pick of the litter."

"Well, I am happy to see you too Douglas. I don't see anything wrong with making my move before you come in and sweep all these fine honeys off their feet."

"Well, tonight won't be that night John. This week I met this fine high yellow. She was stunning. I was smitten by her."

"Smitten, Douglas Brown is smitten by a woman. I thought you had dedicated your life to spanking as many women as you can. What happen to "I will never let another woman break my heart like MiYong did?"

"John, that rule is still in force; however, I guess there are some females left out there that can catch your attention."

"Well, I guess there are."

"Besides, I am not really smitten. She just caught my eye."

"Anyway Douglas, you should never forget the golden rule."

"What rule is that John?"

"Never pee where you sleep."

"What? I believe the rule is never play where you work."

"Whatever Douglas, that is a good rule too but right now, I need to turn my attention to the sweet thing I was talking to before you interrupted me."

"Okay John, go ahead and have fun. I need to get home early tonight. I'll talk to you later."

As the night progressed, John was able to convince that "sweet young thing" as he called her to leave with him. I had thoughts of Ann on the brain and didn't feel up to getting my spank on. I soon left and drove home thinking about Ann.

~ CHAPTER FIVE ~

New Office Visit

Moving time came quicker than expected. I had the dubious task of coordinating and directing the move of three offices and forty females to the Towers Building. Bellsouth was downsizing its Atlanta organization and consolidating personnel in its southeastern district to one office building. Soon, I would have to give up my corner office where I had a perfect view of the entire city. I also would no longer have the privacy of being in the rear section of the building watching all who came and went for whatever reason. As the moving day came closer, I knew all the ladies would be depending on me for their survival. I was responsible for giving all of my co-workers a tour of the new office location and layout.

To make sure the facility was open and all was in order, I sent Tony Marshall the facility engineer and Tonya Smith the admin clerk over earlier that morning to unlock the doors so everything would be ready when the staff arrived. I had just driven up when I noticed that Tony's car was parked in front of the building. It seemed odd that he would leave his car out front. I tried not to give it much thought; however, there were a lot of parking spaces in the designated parking lot. Maybe he was in a hurry.

As I entered the door, I notice a small package lying on the floor. It had Trojan in big black letters written on it. I quickly picked it up, thinking that it must have dropped out of the pocket of one of the construction workers. I proceeded to walk down the hall when I heard a noise coming from one of the offices. The door was slightly cracked and Tony was sweating like he was in the race of his life. I peeked in the door and there they were. I was not shocked, but I was pleasantly surprised that Tony and Tonya had kept this secret from the rest of the office. I for one was not about to let anyone know that they were a little more than co-workers.

I thought to myself jokingly, if this were a ship we would have a bottle of champagne. But since this was a building, what better way to christen the building. I slowly withdrew and went to the next hallway. I opened one of the doors and slammed it shut very hard. I stood there laughing as I imagine them scrambling to put their clothes on. I wanted to see their faces as the door slamming took them by surprise. I gave them a few minutes to get dressed before I returned to their location, I heard Tony's voice asked in a higher than normal tone.

"Who is here, is that you Mr. Brown?"

I said with a little laughter in my voice, "Yes Tony. Where are you? Is Tonya with you?"

"Yes Sir," he said. I made it around the corner to see both of them standing in the lobby not far from the office where I had just witnessed them performing their missionary service.

"How long have you been here sir?" Tony asked.

"Oh not long," I said as I looked into Tonya's eyes and smiled. I asked them if they have a chance to open up all the new offices and try out the new desks. Tonya's face started to turn red. I quickly changed the subject and asked Tony to move his car from in front of the building to the main parking lot. Both of them left the building in a hurry. As Tonya walked away, I noticed the hem of her dress turned up into her panties. I cleared my throat hoping she would double check herself to make sure everything was ok as she exited the door. What a way to start things off in your new office building.

Shortly afterward, the entire staff arrived. It was a site to behold. My boss, Mr. Green led the tour briefing each of them as he went along. I stayed close to answer any questions they might have. As I was walking, I noticed Ann smiling like she usually does. She was walking with her protector and confidant, Sheila Brown. Sheila protected Ann as if she were the big sister. Ann must have told her the entire story of her divorce. I only knew part of the story. I was leery about talking to Ann concerning her personal life outside the office. I could not possibly chance another encounter like the one I experienced in the technology room. Ann noticed I was looking at her and paused so I could catch up.

"Hi Ann," I said as if I was in grade school getting ready to have my first conversation with a girl.

"Where did you say my office would be Mr. Brown?"

"Oh, it is right across from the Directors office."

"Is that it over there?"

"Yes, it is room number five?"

"So, Mr. Brown I never had the opportunity to thank you for all your help you have given me during my orientation."

"Hey don't mention it. I enjoy making you feel welcome. I guess it is my old fashioned southern up bringing."

"So, where can we go and have lunch?"

"Well, there are several fast food restaurants down the street. When do you want to go?"

"Sheila and I are going after we leave here. Do you want to come with us?"

"Oh no, I have to lock up and make sure everything is secure. I hope the both of you have a great time."

Ann rejoined the tour that was being given by my boss as I felt as though the life was being sucked right out of my bones.

Well, I guess I won't be as lucky as Tony. I thought to myself as I walked slowly behind the group. The things I could do with Ann. No one had a clue of the thoughts that were running through my mind, not even Sheila. It was just her habit of being protective towards Ann. If I did get the opportunity, I would definitely take her home and make mad passionate love to her. It would be just my luck that Sheila would show up telling me that Ann didn't need anyone making mad passionate love to her. Nevertheless, I need to play my cards right until she gets over her last relationship.

~ Chapter Six ~

Temptation

The next day at the main office, time was flying. All of the ladies were coming by or calling me asking mega questions. I told them that they only needed to pack their files, put their office number on the boxes and I would take care of the rest. I had already put their names on each door located at the new office. They didn't have to do anything else.

During the afternoon, I had to visit one of our satellite offices. I needed to take inventory of all the furniture and equipment. I had called Flora Cannon at the Decatur field office to let her know I was coming by. When I arrived, there were no other cars but hers in the parking lot. I knocked on the door so I wouldn't startle her. Flora was in the bathroom taking care of some business. I announced my presence again to make sure she had everything intact when she exited the bathroom. Flora was an attractive female in her early forties. She ruled her office with an iron hand.

"Hello Douglas," she said while I was looking behind one of the filing cabinets to read the serial number.

"Hi Flora," I said smiling while giving her the once over.

"Do you see something you like Douglas?"

"I see a lot I like, but it belongs to someone else."

"But, it could belong to you if you weren't so afraid."

"I am not afraid Flora. I have tamed horses wilder than you."

"Well, put on your spurs and trot over here."

I turned to see the most amazing site, nestled slightly below her navel button. I must admit the invitation was tempting.

"Girl, you better put that away before somebody gets hurt."

She just smiled.

"I knew you were a scared man. I offer you a golden opportunity and you run like a rabbit. I bet Tony wouldn't run if I offered it to him."

"From what I have heard and seen, Tony can handle himself." I let out a little laughter.

"I am just kidding Flora. If you weren't taken by Mr. Tuesday I would have you smoking like a pork roast on a slow cooker. As tempting as it is, I don't think you can handle what I could do for you."

She started towards me to call my bluff. Outside, we heard a car parking in the gravel parking lot. She quickly put her brilliance back underneath her dress and sat down at her desk. A few minutes, later Tony opened the door.

"You beat me again boss."

"Yes I did. However, this time I was glad to do so."

"Hi Flora," Tony said as he went into the next room to start inventorying the equipment.

"You see Douglas, Tony would have done right by a girl and thought nothing of it."

"I know Flora. Let me tell you a story about why I don't want you to get caught up with what I have to offer. A few years ago, I had the opportunity to have as many women as I wanted. I was a stud and knew it. White women loved me, Oriental women adored me and Black women couldn't get enough of me. One night I was at this club in Germany. It was a slow night. The lights were so low that they cast shadows in the corners of the back rooms. I met this German babe. She had silky long black hair and a body to match. Her name was Monica. She was fine as can be. Monica told me that she was just waiting on a man like me to fulfill her fantasies. After a few drinks, we moved to a table that was located in one of the dark corners. She told me that she had never made love in a club before. Well, come to think of it I had never made love in a club either."

"It all smells like crap to me Douglas!"

"Just hold on Flora. Let me finish the story. We begin to kiss soft and smooth. Her lips pressed against mine like a soft piece of fruit. I massaged her tongue with my lips, pulling it in next to mine until both of our tongues moved together in a dance. She grabbed me and pressed her body hard against mine. I just held her close until she was consumed by my love."

"Dam, Douglas! I offer you this and you tell me a story about a German woman! You are lucky as hell that Tony showed up."

"Please, are you going to let me finish Flora? I took her home that night and did what any knowledgeable black man would do. We spent the night getting to know each other a little better, if you know what I mean. However, after that, I couldn't get rid of Monica. I thought it was only a chance encounter. You see Flora, I don't want the same to happen to you."

"Douglas! I am all about show, ask Tony."

"Yes, I know you are all about show. If I permitted you, I would have been another one of your victims. You should be glad I didn't take you up on your offer. You would be lying there on the floor or sitting in your chair unable to move."

"Douglas, if I wanted a fairy tale I would have gone to the children's section in the library."

"Yes, I know Flora. If I really wanted a sex slave I wouldn't have told you the story."

By the time Flora and I had finished talking Tony came in the room laughing.

"I didn't know you were so cavalier Mr. Brown."

"Well Tony, I don't get around as much as you but I have tamed a few wild horses in my day."

"You go Mr. Brown!"

"The both of you need to finish up so I can get back to work," said Flora.

Tony and I soon finished our inventory and left Flora's office. I made sure Tony and I left at the same time. I didn't want Tony to receive the spoils of my conversation with Flora.

~ CHAPTER SEVEN ~

Shelia's Excitement

Sheila had a big smile on her face all morning. She kept going into Ann's office laughing and running around like a chicken with her head cut off. She really caught my attention. I had to know what was up. As I headed to Ann's office, Sheila cut me off about the same time that Ann came out of her office with her purse in hand.

"Where are you going Ann?" I asked with excitement in my voice?

"Sheila and I are going to look at some fabric."

"Yes, some fabric. Why is it that every time Ann comes out of her office you bring your big head around sniffing at her?"

"No, it is not that at all. I heard you laughing so loudly that I was intrigued by the commotion."

"Well, you can stop being so intrigued by the commotion because you have waited too late."

"What do you mean I have waited to late? I am too late for what?"

Both of them scurried out of the door laughing together. Well, what was that all about? I walked back to the big window to see Ann and Sheila still smiling as they got into Ann's car. What was the big deal? It's not like I am in Ann's office twenty four seven. I only come by on occasion to relax and have a civil conversation. Well, what ever it is I know it will come to light sooner or later.

"Douglas, can you come to my office for a minute?" As I turned around, I saw Mattie Crenshaw standing in the hallway with her hands placed on her side like she was a little girl.

"I am having problems loading my files into the container you gave me."

"I don't see how you can have a problem. The box takes to size files, legal and letter. You either place them the long way or the short way."

Mattie Crenshaw couldn't do a thing by herself. She was a total pain in the butt. She was always saying, Douglas this, Douglas that. It was enough to make me want to quit my job and become a monk.

"Look here Mattie, you put your letter files this way and your legal file that way. Don't try to put the legal and letter files in the same box."

"Oh you are mad at me," said Mattie in her usual baby voice.

"No I am not mad. I just think you should be able to figure out these simple tasks by yourself. You should not be getting flustered all the time. When you find yourself stuck, step back and look at your problem from another angle. It is my job to make things easer for you; however, I just want you to start making some positive steps in the right direction."

"Ok, thank you," said Mattie. I left her office knowing that this wasn't the last time I would be needed.

When I returned to my office, I once again started to think about Ann and her big secret. What in the world was going on? Had she met someone and I had not picked up on it? We had been working together for eighteen months. I normally can tell when there is a change in someone's life. Maybe I'm slipping or maybe I have waited to late to let my intensions known. Has Ann found someone to fill the void in her life? Well, it won't do me any good sitting here thinking about it. I will ask her later when Sheila is not around. It would be difficult asking any questions when Sheila is there staring you in the face, ready to whip you with one of those quick remarks of hers. I need to get Ann alone. Maybe I can take her out to lunch when we get to the new office location. The only thing I need to do is build up the courage to ask her. I have been tentative about being alone with her since the encounter that day in the technology room.

There have been many days I've sat here in my office daydreaming about what I would do if I had the opportunity to take Ann out on a date. If I did get lucky, I would pick her up at 7:00 presenting her with a bouquet of fresh roses. We would proceed to the Fox Theater in downtown Atlanta to attend a play. I would hold her hand the entire time. Once the play ended we would have dinner at one of the local restaurants. Yes, maybe Gladys Knight's and Ron's restaurant Chicken and Waffles. Afterwards, we would go dancing at Club Legacy. I would hold her in my arms all night long. I would look into her eyes so she could see how much I loved her. She would know that love pervades inside of me. I would tell her why her love is so wonderful that it makes me want to cry. I would tell her why love fills the inside of me, why it gives me joy, pain and misery. I would tell her that her love unlocks the sensitive side of my soul. It gives me courage and makes me bold. I would look her in the eyes and say, what is love that I only think of you. It is a tingling feeling that penetrates me through and through. What is love, but the gift that you give? I would say I will love you today and for as long as you live. Yes, that is what I would do if I weren't so afraid of asking her out but I think it maybe to late.

~ Chapter Eight ~

The Secret

"What do you think Sheila? Is this color a nice shade of white?"

"It is beautiful, who do you have making your dress," Sheila asked?

"Her name is Doris. She is an old friend of the family. She made my first wedding dress. It was simply the bomb. This will be the third time I will walk down the isle. My first marriage lasted five years. I got pregnant during my freshman year in college. I was lucky because I wasn't due until August of that year. No one knew I was pregnant until I got out for summer break. My mother and father were so angry with me. They told me that I would have to work very hard to be successful. I know they were disappointed. However, I was in love. Charles was the love of my life.

Charles and I fell in love during our senior year in high school. We ended up going to the same college. He and I got married after the baby was born. We were set on not letting having a baby interfere with our plans to finish college. I worked hard during the last few months of my freshman year to make A's in all my classes. Charles got a job in downtown Atlanta at the Ritz Carlson as a Bell Hop. He made a lot of tips besides his normal pay. When the baby came, we were set to raise her while going to college. We were both enrolled at Georgia State University and had a little apartment in East Point. It was near Marta so I could travel and take care of things I needed to do. It was easier than I expected.

Once my daughter was old enough, I was able to leave her with Charles' parents Martha and Mathew. Charles' parents were lifesavers. They would baby-sit more than my family would. My mother and sisters worked so much that they could only keep the baby on the weekend. As soon as I could re-enroll, I started my classes. I worked full time and went to school full time. Charles found grant money for both of us. He was so smart. We were a team. Girl, we had a great time. We made love twenty-four-seven. I made sure I was on the pill and when I wasn't he used protection. He had a stockpile of protection he had picked up from the health department. We were so in love.

"Girl I know about that young love."

"Yes, Charles was the man for five years. I knew from time to time when he went out with the guys he probably was seeing someone on the side. Most men did back in the day. I accepted it as long as he didn't bring his business home and it didn't affect our married life.

After five years of marriage he started going away on the weekends. Afterwards, he would receive phone calls and as soon as I would answer, the person on the other end would not say anything. It was a sign that he was seeing someone else.

One afternoon I came home for a quick lunch. I found Charles on the couch in the living room having a snack of his own. I could not believe it. I was stunned. Both of them ran out the back door after I threw the lamp halfway across the room at them. I guess you know I didn't go back to work that day. Five years of marriage! I was Charles' footstool and in one day my life was turned upside down. I didn't see Charles for two days. He didn't dare show his big head around the house. When he finally came home we had a major fight. I got in a few good right jabs. I tried my best to kill him. He could never make up for bringing that "female trash" into my house. He tried to make up for it for a while. Later, he just gave up and continued to see her. We didn't make love any more after that. I finally told him I wanted a divorce. I didn't love him any more and he just needed to go. We had a great life at first and he really helped me to go to school and become independent. So, I guessed things happen for the best."

"Girl, I didn't know. I can tell you a few stories that will knock your socks off. I had several similar situations like you had. That is why I am single now. There was this one guy name Johnny Boy. Johnny Boy could make love like a mule plowing a field all day long. Everyone knew how much I loved Johnny Boy. He was the man in my life. We made love in his car, at his mother's house, at the supermarket, behind the barn and a thousand other places I don't care to repeat. He was the stud of all studs.

The trouble came when this new girl by the name of Sharon was hired down at the club where he worked. I came in the club one Saturday night and found him in the storage room having his way with her. I loved Johnny Boy but I could never get that image out of my mind. I had to let him go. Every now and then he calls to see how I am doing. I let him come over and visit just to pay Sharon back."

"Why?" I asked.

"Well you know he married Sharon."

"Ha, ha," we both laughed as we continued to look at the materials needed to make the wedding dress.

"Now that was revenge at its best Sheila. I just didn't feel the need for revenge. I had to let Charles go. We had been together since high school and I guess he needed to experience love with someone else."

"Yes, I understand what you mean," said Sheila.

"Now that you are getting married, what are you going to do about Douglas."

"What do you mean Sheila?"

"Ann, even a blind women knows that Douglas has been trying to talk to you every since you arrived here a year ago. I don't know what you did to him but he only has the eye for you."

"He has what for me?"

"You know, he wants to talk to you but he doesn't know how."

"I'm so sorry for him. He waited entirely too late. He never expressed that he likes me that way. I think you must have read him wrong. He is just nice to me because of the situation I told him about concerning my ex-husband and me."

"Well, when he hears the news about you getting married, I want you to look at his face. I bet you will be able to drive a tractor truck though his mouth."

"No!!! Ok, may be I am wrong but I don't think so Sheila. Well, we better stop talking about Douglas and get back to work. I still have a week or two to get the fabric. Thanks for helping me Shelia."

"You know you're my girl Ann."

On the way back to the office, I thought to myself about what Sheila had said. Douglas likes me? I don't think so. He is nice but he has never said anything to me that would indicate that he liked me. Besides he is not my type and I don't think I am his type. He has never asked me out to lunch or anywhere else. Sheila is mistaken. If Douglas wanted me he should have asked me out before now. God! I am getting married in two months. Besides he is always teasing with Flora. I know she is dating Mr. Tuesday but they always are going out to lunch or joking with each other. Anyway, it is too late for anyone else. I have found someone who is good to me and he doesn't drink or use drugs. He is a religious man who attends church regularly, loves to sing in the church choir, and has what a women needs when she needs to relax. Sheila must be wrong. If Douglas really likes me, he should have made a move a long time ago. When I get back to the office I will see for myself. If he doesn't make a positive move in my direction without my serious help, I am not going to give it a second thought.

~ Chapter Nine ~

Douglas' Quandary

Its two o'clock. Where are they?"

They should have been back thirty minutes ago. I can't wait too long. I need to get their equipment and furniture packed and loaded by the movers. It will take a while before they can put it on their carts to take over to the new office. Just then, Tony appeared.

"Have you seen Ann and Sheila? They still haven't marked their boxes?"

"No sir, the last time I saw Ann and Sheila they were headed out to lunch."

"Thanks Tony, we need to get started making sure everything is packed and that the movers have marked all the boxes and furniture correctly."

"Ok sir, I will start in the back office and meet you in the middle."

"Okay Tony, I need to finish up some paperwork for the movers and I will meet you."

Fifteen minutes later Ann came into office.

"Hello Douglas."

"Ann!"

"I didn't mean to startle you."

"Oh no, I'm sorry. I was just deep in thought about the move."

"Yes I understand," Ann said.

"Tony said you were looking for me."

"Yes, you and Sheila are the only two I haven't checked off my list. I just needed to verify that everything is ok and you know what office you are assigned too."

"Every thing is ok Douglas. I have boxed up all my files and I am all yours. I mean I am ready for you to move me. Move my office."

"Dam, I said quietly. "Was that an invitation?"

"Douglas, did you say something?"

"No Ann, I was just thinking out loud. As soon as the movers get here we will start loading your office and go from there. You need to collect your things and go to the new office."

"Ok Douglas. Is that all?"

"Yes, Ann, that is all I had."

Ann turned to leave my office and stopped briefly. She leaned her head to the side as if she wanted to turn and ask me a question. She shook her head and continued to walk away. I froze! I froze! She put the carrot out there and I didn't bite it. I should have closed the door and took her into my arms and told her that I loved her. I probably will never have an opportunity like that again. We were all alone in my office! I could have easily spilled my feeling all over her. If only I had another chance. I would tell Ann.

Love is you. It is the sparkle in your eyes that sways my heart. It is that same magic that causes me to smile. Love is your touch. It is the beginning of life. Love is your kiss, capturing me with desire. You cause my mind to race with the wind. I become spellbound and under your complete control. Love is your arms holding me close.

It is the place I want to be, sharing my life stories. Love is your presence. It is your scent upon my face. It is your hair in the breeze. It is your body together with mine. It is the heat that is created in me. Love is your heart beating next to mine, both in rhythm at the same time. Love is your hands caressing my face, giving me strength to welcome each day. Love is your breath upon my lips. Love is my eyes seeing you, knowing that I can love and be loved. Love is watching you walk in and out of my life each day, hoping that I will have a private moment to say, "Love is you."

If I get another chance I will tell her this after the move. As I turned around, I saw Sheila.

"Wake up! Ann doesn't want you anyway," said Sheila.

"What do you mean, I don't like Ann?"

"Well, why are you setting in your chair with your arms folded across each other saying, "Ann love is you?"

"That is not what I am doing Sheila."

"Yes it is. Your head is so far up Ann's butt you can see inside her pelvis."

"What do you need Sheila?"

"I don't need anything. Tony told me you were looking for me. I know you Douglas. You just wanted to see what Ann and I were doing at lunch."

"No I don't Sheila. Why do you always feel the need to keep me in check?"

"Because, it is what I do best," said Sheila.

"You had your chance and blew it Douglas. You are a year late and a dollar short. However, you can always go and play with Flora."

"No thank you. I rather live all alone."

"Well, you better get use to it." Sheila smiled arrogantly and left out of the office.

I was stunned. I could not believe I was acting out a fantasy. Of all people, how could I let Sheila catch me daydreaming about Ann. Now, I will never be able to tell Ann how I feel. Sheila is probably in there right now opening her big mouth.

"Sir, the movers are here," said Tony.

"Thanks, Tony. I know I said I would meet you, I just have been a little busy."

"No problem sir, I took care of everything. I checked Sheila's and Ann boxes too. We are ready to move."

"Great! I will get the movers."

"Good afternoon Mr. Brown," said Dan White the crew supervisor for the moving company Parker and Packers.

"We are ready to start packing."

"How do you do sir," I said while still in deep thought about the conversation I had with Sheila.

"This is Tony, he will be here at this location to answer any questions you may have. Everything is ready to go Mr. White. Your team can load up and I will be back and forth checking on things. I need to go to the new office and make sure everything is being set up properly. Do you have my cell phone number?"

"Yes, Mr. Brown I do," said Dan.

"Tony, if you have any questions you can call me on my cell phone, Okay."

"Yes Sir, Mr. Brown," Tony said jokingly. No one called me Mr. Brown except Tony. I guess it was odd to hear me referred to in that way.

On the way out of the office, I noticed Ann and Sheila leaving the building just laughing their heads off. I felt like a big fool. I just knew that Sheila was telling Ann everything she heard me say. Now I will never be able to face her with the truth of my heart. By the time I reached the steps outside, they were driving away. It seemed to be an indication of what I was to be. I know I dug this hole in my life by not giving any women an opportunity to screw my life up again. So now, I might as well live with my decision.

~ Chapter Ten ~

Ann's Marriage

By the end of the week, everyone had moved to the new office location. I was enjoying my new furniture and new surroundings. Sheila and I had received the best possible treatment from Douglas. He always made me feel like I was a priority in the work place. Everyone really enjoyed the new facility. I was glad because I would soon be taking time off to get married. It was a decision I made quickly. Robert Peterman was a senior executive at Barns and Hurst Advertising Agency. He managed several of their biggest accounts. I fell in love the day he first kissed me. He was a man that knew what he wanted and what he wanted was me. He was a perfect gentleman each time we went out on a date. He never once tried to make love to me. He said he wanted to wait until we got married. Now, there were a few times I wanted and needed him to take me and square a sister up! However, he helped me through the situation with a gentle stroke of his loving hand. At times it is hard not to want him. I just meditate and think about when I will be able to make love to him in every room in the house. I am going to be the best wife in the world.

"Ann, are you in there?" asked Sheila.

"Yes, I am. Please come in. The office door is not locked."

"We are getting ready to go to lunch. Do you want to go?"

"Yes, I would love too. Who else is going?"

"The six of us are going, Cynthia, Flora, Tonya and Melissa."

"Ok Sheila let me get my sweater."

"Come on you two, we have been waiting here forever," said Melissa.

"We're coming Melissa," shouted Sheila.

The six of us got into Flora's car and drove to Applebee's. This was one of my favorite restaurants. I enjoyed their salmon salad and for desert I always had the fried cheesecake with ice cream. It was simply delicious.

"Ann, what are you daydreaming about," asked Flora?

"It better not be anybody I know."

"No Flora, it is not about anyone you know. I don't think my honey and you run in the same circle."

"What do you mean by that Ann Taylor," said Flora in a harsh tone.

"I didn't mean anything. I was just daydreaming about my boyfriend."

"Oh, Ann got a boyfriend, they all said in unison.

"A boyfriend!" When did you have time to get a boyfriend," asked Cynthia.

"Hold that thought until we get inside."

"Okay, I will tell you a little news. I am pretty excited."

"No Ann, let me tell," asked Sheila.

We parked the van and entered the restaurant. There was a cozy booth on the left side. I could not wait to sit down and order. I was starving.

"Waitress," I bellowed as quickly as I could. I would like to order the salmon salad."

"The salmon salad, yes that will be great," said Cynthia.

Flora ordered a fried chicken salad, Tonya and Melissa ordered a rib basket and Sheila ordered a Caesar salad.

"Okay, tell me about this boyfriend of yours."

"Well he is a little more than a boyfriend," said Sheila.

"Sheila, that is all they need to know, said Ann.

"Okay I will keep my big mouth shut."

"Well ladies you will find out soon enough but you must not tell anyone else at work."

"Okay we won't," said all of them.

"I am getting married next week."

"You are what!" said Cynthia.

"Yes, I am getting married next week. I know this is a big surprise to all of you. However, I did not want a big wedding. I am having a small ceremony at my mother's and that will be that. I met someone who I feel I can spend the rest of my life with. I am not getting any younger. All of you have someone or is hiding someone in your life. I don't need to date a long time. I need to be with the man I love every day and not just on the weekends. I will soon be the next Mrs. Robert Peterman. "

"Well, that is just fine by me. Good luck and good by. Maybe now I can corner that scared chicken of a man Douglas Brown. I finally don't have to worry about him looking in your direction anymore," said Flora.

"What do you mean?" asked Ann?

"Now I know you are not that dumb. Douglas has been trying to find the right way to ask you out to lunch for at least a year."

"I didn't have a clue. I thought he was just being nice. You know how he is."

"Yes he is nice; however, he is nicer to you. Everyone knows if Ann asks for something, Douglas will run and get it. If I want something, he will send Tony to get it. So you see Ann there is a real difference between being nice and being nice."

Flora started to laugh causing everyone else to laugh too. Sheila looked at me with a big fat "I told you so" grin on her face. I just sat there thinking. I had given Douglas a couple of opportunities to say something. He never really asked any questions along the line of would you like to go to lunch or what are you doing this evening. I just figured that he was nice to me, like if I was the teacher's pet. I never thought that he had the type of feeling that Flora and Sheila mentioned.

He waited to late. For all I care, he can like Flora or whomever he wants. He is just a friend and I have Robert in my life now. Robert made the right move and captured my heart. Douglas only captured my friendship.

"Wake up Ann, to late to daydream about Douglas," said Melissa.

"All this time Ann has been letting us think she was the belle of the ball and what happened to her in her last marriage made her timid and withdrawn. Now, look at her. She is getting ready to jump the broom again. How many brooms will you have now in your closet?" asked Melissa.

"Be nice," said Sheila giving Melissa the evil eye.

"Don't worry Sheila. Melissa is harmless. This will make the third broom I have in my closet and if you get out of line I will take one out and sweep you up side the head."

"Girl, you know I don't have a problem with that. I am just making conversation. Each of you already knows I got married last year."

"Yes we know."

"Jeff is a fireman with DeKalb County. Last Friday night when I came home he had cooked me salmon and laid it over a beautiful spinach salad. It was delicious. Afterward he went upstairs and changed into his black silk pajama bottoms. He came and stood at the bottom of the steps and asked me if I wanted to pass. I still had on my tight skirt and my silk t-shirt I had worn to work. He just stood there like a replica of an African warrior. His spear was long and intimidating. I fell at his feet and asked permission to pass. He said yes. I paid homage to his spear by placing my hands upon its firmness acknowledging its great strength and power. Afterward, we went up stairs, so I may ascend to the mount of Jeff where I was compelled to ride the horse of forbidden passion until I broke him. After about three minutes, that horse was broke, but the dam salmon salad was delicious."

"Girl, you are too crazy. I will tell you a story." said Cynthia.

"Just last night, my baby was lying in bed waiting for me to get out of the shower. When I came in, he didn't have any clothes on. He was lying on the bed. He had written a poem and started to read it as I approached. Would each of you like to hear it? "

"OK," said everyone.

"It is titled Body and Soul. It reads.

"I feel your lips pressing against mine.

Our embrace seems to last forever.
I see your eyes looking into mine.
You summon my love to come forth.
I feel your hands touching mine.
Your power causes me to erupt.
I feel your chest touching mine.
I am consumed by your passion and desire.
I feel your body joined with mine.
You are deep within my soul
and forever we become a part of love itself."

"Dam!" said Sheila.

"Does someone have a wet nap? All of this talk about love, marriage, and poetry is making a sister hot. I could tell all of you a story that would knock your panties off. But we don't have time. We need to finish eating and go back to work."

"You're right Sheila," I said.

"Well don't, please don't tell anyone else at the office I am getting married. I'll let them know when I return from my honeymoon."

"Okay," everyone said reluctantly. On the drive back to work, I sat in the back seat with Sheila and Flora. I started to wonder if what everyone said about Douglas was true. There was nothing I could do now, because my heart belonged to Robert.

After we arrived back at work, everyone was still busy setting up there new offices. Tony was assisting Tonya hanging pictures and a bulletin board. I started to enter my office and noticed Douglas was going over the inventory. He raised his head for a moment and smiled politely. It seemed to me that he didn't have any feelings. Shelia suddenly appeared.

"I caught you Ann!"

"What do you mean?" I asked.

"You wanted to see if it was true."

"If what was true?" I asked Sheila.

"Does Douglas really like you?"

"Well, I know he likes me but I don't think he likes me in the way you think."

"We will see, here he comes."

"Hey Ann, Sheila," said Douglas.

"Go away boy, you waited a year too late" said Sheila.

"Yea, you waited too late." I said.

I didn't know what or why I said what I did. I was just following Sheila. Douglas must have thought we were crazy. He walked away shaking his head. Sheila started to laugh.

"Maybe he doesn't like you. I bet we will see after you get married."

"Good bye Sheila," I said. I need to concentrate on organizing my office."

"Good bye Ann," Sheila said leaving my office.

After I finished organizing my office, I decided to write Douglas a letter explaining why I got married. It would make me feel better that he understood. I did not want to return to work knowing he was hurt. I didn't know what to say or where to start. I just needed to be honest with him and let him know how much I have enjoyed being his friend.

~ Chapter Eleven ~

Doomsday

The movers had finally left after a week of relocating into the new building. Everyone was finishing setting up their office to fit their particular drama. I was still busy making sure all of the equipment was functioning properly after being banged around by the movers. Everything for the most part was okay. I had taken the liberty a week ahead of time to ensure my priority equipment was set up so we would not have any problems Monday morning when every one returned to their office. I had spent the weekend pulling equipment from this office to that office so I wouldn't hear thirty screaming females trying to ask me where their precious little table or chairs were. Mondays were bad enough as it were. I did not need anyone to come to work missing seven days out of thirty. You know what I mean, that time of the month. Females can be quite testy.

By Wednesday, everyone except Ann had came back to work. I had not seen Ann for two days. The last time I saw her was in her office with Sheila several days ago. I guess Ann decided to take a few days off.

"Hello Douglas."

"Hello Sheila," I said meeting her as she exited the coffee room.

"Have you seen Ann this week?"

"Douglas, I guess no one told you."

"Told me what?"

"Ann is gone on her honeymoon."

"On her honeymoon, when did she get married?"

"She got married last Saturday," Shelia said with a small grin on her face.

I stood there trying to recover from the shock. As I walked away to go back to my office, Shelia grabbed me by my hand and held it as if I was a little child.

"Now, don't you cry, Douglas? You are a big boy."

I pulled my hand away trying to play the bad news down.

"What do you mean? Most people would let their friends know that they were getting married. I guess she is not expecting to receive a wedding gift from me. What type of friend in their right mind would run off and get married without telling their co-workers. I have tried to make Ann feel welcome. In my mind, I thought to myself that I had waited too late to tell her I how I truly feel. This marriage thing came as a complete shock to me. I thought after the break-up with her last husband she would wait for two or three years. Some folks would say that he married her on the rebound. It is tough when that happens. Some marriages don't make it. I felt sick to my stomach. I kept hearing her over and over in my mind saying, "Yes, I do. "Yes I do."

Well, I guess that is what happens when a fellow tries to wait for the right opportunity. He gets left out in the cold.

"Knock, Knock."

"Who is it?

"Flora!

"What do you want?"

"I don't want too much, I just came to see if you were ok. Sheila called and told me she gave you the bad news."

"So you knew too?"

"Yes sweetie, we all knew."

"Even Tony?" I asked.

"No, none of the men knew, only the five of us knew. We found out a few weeks ago while having lunch. Ann did not want to make a big deal about it. It was just Sheila, Cynthia, Tonya, Melissa and I. Don't feel bad. We told Ann you had a crush on her. She didn't have a clue that you liked her. Come and give mama a hug."

"Well, thank you very much Flora, but I don't need a hug. What I need is to be left alone so I can do the work I have scheduled for today."

"Okay Douglas, but now you don't have any excuse."

"Any excuse for what?" I asked.

"To stop being a scared chicken shit man," she said laughing while leaving my office.

I guess I should have grabbed Flora and gave her what she wanted right in my office. How could I? I was still in shock after hearing the doomsday news. I thought I was closer to Ann than that. I do not understand why she felt like she had to hide the news from me.

"Douglas, Hello, Douglas!"

"Yes, who is it?" I said in a higher than normal tone.

"Cynthia."

I got up out of my chair and made it over to the door and opened it.

"Here," Cynthia said calmly.

"Ann asked me to give you this letter after she went on vacation. She did not want to put it in your mailbox or under your door. By the way I am sorry, about Ann getting married. We all knew you like her a little more than a friend."

"Thanks, I'm okay." I closed the door and fell back in my chair. I took a good look at the letter to see if it was an invitation that arrived too late. It was indeed a letter. As I opened it, my heart started to beat faster. I didn't know what to expect. She had used office stationary to write me a two page letter. It read:

Douglas, I don't know where to start. I first would like to say thank you for welcoming me into the office and taking care of me when I was going through a very difficult period in my life. You are the one male I have met in the office that I could come to and was greeted with a smile and true customer service. You made it so easy for me to adjust to my new work surrounding. It is not everyday that a girl meets a man who she can just be friends with. You are that man. I know Sheila gives you a lot of grief sometimes; however, I am glad you are able to recognize she really doesn't mean any harm. On

Saturday, I will be getting married to Robert Peterman. He is a very nice man. I met him shortly after my return to Atlanta. My sister introduced him to me at church. He asked me two months ago to marry him. I had a void that needed to be filled. He has been able to help fill it. So, why am I writing this letter? I consider you a very good friend. A few weeks ago the girls confessed to me that you were sweet on me. Well, to put it simply, they said you really liked me as a woman and wanted to get to know me better. I really didn't think I was slow, but I never picked up on any vibes that you wanted our friendship to be more than what it was. I came to you afterward to check for myself and you did not react to the advance I made. So, I guess what I am saying is that I hope you understand that I made this decision not knowing your feelings or if you really had any feelings for me. When I return to work, I will be a different person name wise but I will always be your friend and co-worker. Love, Ann.

Inside, I started to cry but I knew it was my entirely my fault that she had married this man. She was right. I hadn't made one move in her direction to tell her how I really felt. I guess I just have to lick my wounds and move on. I am a big boy and can have any woman I desire. But no one can replace Ann Taylor or should I say Ann Peterman. I will always have her in a special place.

~ Chapter Twelve ~

The New Kid on the Block

"Good morning," said Stephanie as she stood in front of the receptionist desk looking like a gift from God.

"Can I help you?" asked Sheila?

"Yes, I am here to interview with Cynthia Brannon."

"Okay, please come in and have a seat."

I could not believe my eyes. I was blown away for a minute.

"Hello," she said as she sat down in a single chair that was along the wall of the reception area. I could not resist introducing myself.

"My name is Douglas," I said with the biggest smile across my face.

"My name is Stephanie Johnson," she said as I tried to make sense of this miracle of nature.

"Do you work for Bellsouth?" I asked.

"No, not yet, but I hope I will be working here soon after my interview with Ms. Brannon."

"I hope so too. I mean I wish you good luck on your interview."

Just then, Sheila interrupted by pushing me out of the way with her hips.

"Excuse me Douglas, Ms. Brannon asked me to show Stephanie into her office."

"Thank you, Douglas."

"Good luck, Stephanie."

Well, I said to myself as I went to the front desk to cover for Sheila while she was away. Just then the receptionist's phone rang. I picked it up and answered it in a professional voice.

"Hello, you have reached Bellsouth southeastern office. How may I direct your call?"

"Sheila, please."

There was no mistaken that voice. It was Ann Taylor or now Ann Peterman. I said calmly, "Ms. Sheila Jordan is not available, would you like to leave a message Mrs. Peterman?"

She froze for a moment. I could here crickets making noise as if no one or nothing else existed.

"No, thank you very much Douglas," as she hung the phone up. I put the phone back on the receiver as a big lump developed in my throat. Again, I acted like some ass out of a stupid movie. I should have wished her the best and congratulated her. Instead, I acted as if I was hurt and jealous. She had the right to be happy. If not with me, with whomever she wanted.

"Thanks Douglas for watching the phone for me," said Sheila.

"It was no problem," I said.

"Oh by the way, Ann called. She didn't leave a message. She hung up before I had an opportunity to pull my head out of my ass."

Sheila just smiled and let me kick myself for once.

As I started to walk back toward my office, I saw Cynthia and Stephanie walking toward the coffee room. It looked to me like Cynthia had already made up her mind about hiring Stephanie.

"Wow" I thought to myself. It would indeed be a pleasure to have some new blood in the office. However, I was still feeling bad about Ann but this could be the medicine that the doctors ordered to cure me of my broken heart. As I got closer to my office Cynthia stopped me and made an introduction.

"Douglas, this is Stephanie Johnson."

"Well, hi again Stephanie Johnson, I guess the luck I wished for you paid off."

"I guess so Mr. Brown."

"Douglas," I said without hesitation.

"Thanks, she said as Cynthia started to give her the run down of my job.

"Well you see, Douglas handles about all there is to handle. If you have any questions feel free to see him for all your operational needs."

"Cynthia, don't forget to schedule time for me to brief Stephanie on all the policies and procedures for the operational side of things. I want to make sure I cover everything with her."

Cynthia thought to herself, "Isn't that great." Mr. Douglas Brown has taken a personal interest in someone else. I guess Ann has been moved to the third spot around here."

"Okay Douglas, I will call you this afternoon to arrange a briefing for Stephanie."

"Ok," I smiled and continued to my office. I did notice the curve that stood on the left and right sides of Stephanie's body. But I made a pledge to look and admire and not go any further than that. If I didn't let Ann know how I really felt about her, I am not going to let my emotions run wild about Stephanie.

The next week came soon enough. Still there was no Ann. She had taken two weeks off instead of one week for her wedding and honeymoon. I was still a little confused about the suddenness of the whole thing. I had to get over it and move on. Ann and I would always be good friends. She really enjoyed my friendly disposition and I enjoyed paying her compliments.

"Knock, knock."

"Come in," I said as I turned to see Stephanie peeping through the door.

"Good morning," she said as my male hormones started to take on a character of their own. This was a little different than when I met Ann for the first time. Stephanie was a "young thang", in her early thirties.

"Well, hello Ms. Johnson. How is your orientation going?

"It is going fine Douglas. I wanted to ask you if you have time to give me a briefing about your area of responsibility. Cynthia had to attend an impromptu meeting."

"I was a little busy, but for you I can take a break and finish my portion of your orientation."

"Thank you so much Douglas."

"Well, where do I start? I am Douglas Brown, the southeastern operations manager for Bellsouth. My job is to coordinate facilities and equipment resources to support each department. You just need to submit the required forms that Cynthia briefed you on and I will do the rest. There is equipment you request quarterly and other equipment you request on a weekly basis. This is the only way I can guarantee its availability. You are required to sign out all equipment. If you need supplies, you must fill out a form and allow for proper pickup and distribution. As you see, it is quite simple to get what you need if you plan. My door is always open to provide you support."

"Do you really mean that Douglas?" Stephanie asked.

"Yes I do. So tell me Stephanie, are you really from California."

"Yes, I was born and raised there. My mother was born in Georgia and suggested I move here after my recent divorce. So I sold my house and packed up my things with my four kids and moved here. I purchased a house five miles from my mom's."

"That must be nice," I said.

"Yes it is. I can still maintain my independence and have my mother close by. I need this job to supplement my child support."

"So, how do you like living here so far?"

"It's okay. My kids are getting use to their schools and I am getting use to the Atlanta traffic. It is not too bad. California traffic is worst. As long as I have my mother's support I will be okay. She helps me with babysitting a lot."

"So what do you do for fun?"

"I like to work out. A girl doesn't have a body like this if she does not work out."

"Yes, I guess you are right about that. It is a nice body. Oh, I am sorry that slipped out."

"You know Douglas, Tony said the same thing."

"Tony would, it is his profession."

"Oh, stop teasing Douglas."

"I am not teasing. Tony is a man on the prowl. He will eat anything that gets in his way. I am sorry. I think it is best that we get away from this conversation. If you need me for anything just drop by my office and I will see if I can help you. Just remember the pecking order. My boss is number one, and Ann is number two."

"Oh, can I be number three?"

"We will see."

"Thanks a million Douglas. I know you were busy and you took the time to brief me."

"No problem. Anytime you have questions please come by."

"Okay," Stephanie said as she walked out of my office.

I could not resist looking at her young fine body. It has a bounce that drew you in with every step she took. She was going to be difficult to work around.

On Tuesday, I arrived at work at 7:30. It was close to my normal arrival time. I enjoyed getting to work early so I could make sure everything was ready prior to the employee's arrival. At 7:45, Tony came knocking at my door.

"Mr. Brown, have you talked to Stephanie yet?"

"Yes I have, Tony."

"Isn't she the bomb? I talked with her at break yesterday in my office. While we were talking she put her hands on her skirt and rotated it all the way around. I was shocked. It was amazing. She didn't even blink an eye. She just smiled at me and kept talking."

"Well you know Tony, she is from California. They are more open about life than we are in the south. I wouldn't think anything of it."

"I know sir, but she is fine as can be."

"That is the truth but aren't you involved with Tonya."

"What do you mean, Mr. Brown?"

"Well before we moved over here I observed you and Tonya in one of the offices doing what gown-ups do. You had her feet pointing up toward the ceiling tiles."

"Mr. Brown, someone had to christen the new building."

"So that is what it is called now–a-days."

"I guess Tonya felt special being the first to be christened in the new building.

"Do you have the same plans for Stephanie?"

"Mr. Brown, I think you have that job tied up. From what I hear, you and Stephanie have been looking kind of hard at each other."

"Nonsense," I am the operations manager and that is all. She is nice but I don't want to get involved for a while."

"Isn't it time you got over Ann? She is married now and from what I here you never had a chance."

"I guess you are right, Tony. I might as well get busy living. Ann will be back soon and I need to have my stuff in order."

"Okay, Mr. Brown. I didn't mean to get into your business. I just had to ask if you had met Stephanie."

"I know, Tony. You have a good day."

"I will, Mr. Brown."

The next day, I had left my door open while I was down the hall checking on a new telephone that had been installed in a vacant office. When I returned, I was surprised to see Stephanie sitting in my chair smiling like a kid that just received a lollipop. I have to admit, I want to be the lollipop that she had received.

"Hello, Douglas I thought I would take you up on your offer."

"Well, tell me what offer was that?"

"You said, if I needed anything I need only come by your office. Well, I need to use your computer to surf the web for a street location where I need to attend training today. All the other computers are tied up."

"Go right ahead, you seem to have everything at your disposal."

I must admit she was a beautiful piece of eye candy. She was very lucky that she did not fall within the "I just have to have you" range for me. However, I decided to play along with her to see how far she would go.

"Douglas!" Stephanie shouted in a higher than normal tone.

"Yes Stephanie, I am sorry. I dosed off for a moment."

"Where is Map Quest on this computer?"

"It is under 'My Favorites.' Let me show you."

"Okay thanks, you are so nice to me."

"Well, I just can't help myself. There you go. What time do you have to go to your training?"

"I have to be there by 11:00 am."

"Well, if you need anything else just let me know."

"I will, Douglas."

Boy old boy, why did I have to put that clause in my contract? You know the "look but don't touch" clause. I guess it is all for the best. I still remember how I got caught up in my last relationship. It is always the good guy who ends up with a broken heart. I thought I was with someone who really loved me. I just don't think I can trust anyone one with my heart. So, I will let the games begin and play it like a pro. I deserve to have a little fun. If I don't Tony, will try and lay her across a desk somewhere with her feet pointing straight up in the air. Better me than him.

~ Chapter Thirteen ~

Second Fiddle

Good morning Sheila," I said while attempting to navigate the newly installed metal detector. I must have been the last employee to walk through because none of the lights were on.

"What happened here?" I asked.

"Girl, Douglas has gone "ape shit" while you were on leave. After President Bush declared war on Afghanistan, Douglas has secured the office from top to bottom. He needs to take this contraption and stick it up his ass!"

"Be nice, Sheila. It can't be that bad."

"I guess you are right, Ann. However, it still would be nice to see Douglas with this contraption up his butt."

"Well, that would be funny; however, I don't think we would get any support from him."

"Okay."

"Call me when you get to your office Ann. I want to hear all about the wedding and your honeymoon."

"Okay, Sheila but first I need to get settled and brought up-to-date on the current accounting activities. Did you know I called you while I was on leave?"

"I know. Douglas told me."

"It is so very expensive to call from Cancun. After hearing Douglas' voice, I just hung up. I didn't want to talk to him while I was on my honeymoon. I felt like I was cheating."

"I understand girl, but you don't have to worry about Douglas any more. While you were out, Cynthia hired this sweet little girl. She has been keeping Douglas busy. Every time I look up, she is in his office. I believe you are no longer number two around here."

"Well, that will be just fine with me."

The phone rang.

"Okay, Ann let me catch this call. Don't forget to call me after you have settled in."

"I will Sheila."

On the way to my office, I felt a little uneasy. I don't know why. I really didn't owe anyone an explanation about my unannounced marriage. It was my personal affair and I have the right to keep it that way.

Seconds later, I soon arrived at my door and attempted to open it before anyone else knew I was back. It was like I opened my door and an alarm went off. Cynthia, Tonya and Melissa came pouring into my office. I hardly had time to set my purse down before Melissa started to ask questions about the marriage and the honeymoon. Cynthia started to spill the beans about her new employee and Douglas. I told all of them to wait.

"I just got back! I will go to lunch with you later and we can all get reacquainted."

"Okay girl, no need to get your panties in a bunch. We know when we are not loved," said Melissa.

"Yea, we are just excited to see you."

"You know as soon as Sheila sees you we won't be able to get a word in edge wise," said Cynthia.

All of them started to laugh as they departed my office. Sheila and I were friends but we were not close friends. We hardly ever talked outside the office. I probably had the same level of friendship with all of them.

Great! Now I can sit down for a moment and read my emails and review the calendar of events for the next two weeks. It didn't take but half the morning to accomplish my re-introduction back into the accounts receivable department. I felt a lot better "being in the know." I was caught up with activities and could now make plans for the new collections department that was near completion.

As I finished reading the last of my emails, I noticed Douglas had sent me a welcome back Internet card. It was from one of the "send-a-card internet sites." It read.

When I am with you
the sun opens the heavens
and starts each day.
It feels like the first time
my heart has been opened to love.
When I am with you,
flowers start to bloom.
They release their fragrance
at the exact moment you pass by.
They know that someone special
is near them.
When I am with you,
my heart has a different beat.
My spirit dances to music
that we can only hear.
Excitement tantalizes our souls.
When I am with you,
birds gather around to see you.
They sing songs to win your favor.
They fly merrily along,
hoping to sit on your finger.
When I am with you,
I feel the calm of the ocean.
Your breath is like a cool breeze upon the sea.
When I am with you,
the earth moves,
letting the world know you are alive.
When I am with you,
Father Time lets us walk along,
and in those brief seconds
We can love each other
as it was meant to be.

At the bottom he wrote, "I hope you and Robert will feel the same way about each other as it is written in the poem."

I was deeply moved. It seems that Douglas had written a poem about my complete feelings for Robert. In some small way the poem finally addressed Douglas' feelings for me. He never told me but I must confess I knew he liked me a little. I just didn't think he had strong feelings for me. The poem somehow released me from any obligations we may have had and now presented us an opportunity to be true friends.

Just then the phone rang. It was Sheila.

"Ann, it is 12:30. I have been waiting on you to call."

"Sheila, I have been very busy. I had to get myself organized. I told the other ladies I would meet them for lunch. Are you ready to go?"

"Yes, you can ride with me."

"Okay, let me call Melissa and Cynthia."

"Have you seen Flora?"

"No I guess she is off today or out in the field."

I called Cynthia and told her to get Melissa and meet us at Applebee's. On the way out to meet with Sheila, I saw Douglas talking with someone in his office. He had a very big smile on his face. His mouth was so wide I could see his hometown.

I quickly passed his door and met Sheila outside. I jumped into her car thinking that it was a close one.

"Oh," I said once I was in Sheila's car safely.

"What is wrong with you Ann?"

"Oh, nothing is wrong."

"Something is wrong for you to let out that 'oh', sound."

"Nothing is wrong, Sheila. Can we just go to lunch?"

"Okay, okay, I will take you to lunch.

"So tell me Ann have you seen Douglas since you have been back."

"No, I haven't Sheila."

"I know, Ann. You haven't seen him because of the new girl Stephanie. Every time I look around she is in his office using his computer or setting in one of his chairs having a great old time. Flora came by and caught him talking to her and had a fit. I told her that she should not have made a scene like that but she thought since you were out of the way she would finally get her chance to corner Douglas."

"I don't know why she is still trying to run after guys that don't have an interest in her."

"Sheila, I am a little surprised that Douglas did not come by my office and say hello. Before I went on vacation, I wrote him a long letter explaining why I kept everything a secret. Even if what everyone says about how he feels about me is true. My letter explained everything."

"Well Ann, it seems to me that he has recovered from losing you to Robert and moved on to Stephanie. On the other hand, he probably didn't see you come in. When you go back to the office Douglas will sniff you out like old times. He is probably knocking at your door right now."

"You're probably right."

"So tell me about your wedding."

"I will tell you once we get inside. I don't want to go over it again and again. I will just say that it was a simple wedding but the honeymoon was fabulous."

"Girl, I can't wait," said Sheila.

Once we were inside, we saw Cynthia and Melissa waving at us from our usual corner booth. It seemed we always were able to get the same booth. They took their time to get their orders out before the barrage of questions came.

"Well, welcome back Mrs. Ann Peterman," said Melissa.

"Thank you very much," I said.

I want to thank all of you for the gifts I received. I am glad I told you before I left work what I was going to do. The wedding was a simple affair with just my family and a few of Robert's friends. His parents couldn't make it down. However, we flew up to their hometown two days before we went on our honeymoon. His parents are so nice. They gave us ten acres near a lake on their property.

His father was a little fresh. He kept asking me if I had a sister like me. The second day, I had a long talk with Robert's mother Barbara Peterman. She told me that Robert had been married before. I knew he had. The one thing she was trying to stress is that I needed to know that his previous marriage failed because he spent too much time away from home working. I told her I understood and Robert and I had discussed his job fully. She was happy.

Robert and I spent the rest of our visit enjoying the country and making love under a big oak tree near the lake on his parent's farm. He was so romantic.

"So, whose name is the property in?" asked Shelia.

"It is in Robert's name."

"Well, there you go!"

"What do you mean, Sheila?"

"They want to make sure the property stays in the family."

"Well, I don't have to worry about property Sheila. Robert has a lot of money. What belongs to Robert belongs to me. If Robert and I broke up, I would not want to own property where his family lived any way. Robert has a lot of money and besides I would take all the cash."

We all had a big laugh and paused to eat our salads.

"Now, let me tell the three of you all about my honeymoon. Robert and I flew to Miami the Saturday before our cruise. We celebrated all Saturday night along South Beach. I mean we didn't get in until 3:00 in the morning. We almost missed our cruise the next day. We arrived at the ship when the last call for passengers was made. They almost gave our deluxe cabins to another couple. As soon as we got to our cabins, we locked the door and jumped in the sack. We made love several times before dinner. The first day was simply wonderful. We toured the ship. We played slots. We shopped on board and danced the night away.

On the second day, we ate breakfast in the main ballroom. We ate until we could not put anything else into our mouths. We decide to go topside and walk off some of the food we ate. It was about 2:30 p.m. when we docked at our first port. We arrived in Cancun. It was the most beautiful city in Mexico. We toured the market district collecting little gifts to bring back with us. I have gifts for each of you in my office. You all can pick them up when we go back. Later that evening, we went snorkeling. We laid on the beach and just fell in love all over again. We witnessed the most beautiful sunset as we headed back to the ship. It was great. That night, we ate in the main dinning hall. We had the most wonderful evening with several other couples setting at our table. You know you really had to be there.

On the third day, we docked in Jamaica. The beach was so beautiful. We could see the fish swimming in the dock area. It was totally captivating. Robert and I went scuba diving off the coral peer. We saw so many different and beautiful species of sea life.

When we returned to the boat, we spent the entire evening in the ballroom dancing. It was so romantic. All of the couples that got married on the boat were there with all of the couples that had registered in the honeymoon suite. It was the bomb.

On the last day of our cruise, we docked in the Cayman Islands. We spent all day at the beach. The cruise line had coordinated space for us at the Holiday Inn Resort. We had a great time lying in the sun and taking occasional swims. We kissed so much my lips turned pink. On the way back to the boat, I purchased a rum cake for each of you.

"Even Flora?" asked Sheila.

"She is going to need a rum cake or a bottle of rum. First she couldn't have Douglas because he was stuck on you and now she can't have Douglas because Stephanie has him tied up like a calf in a rodeo."

Everyone had a hardy laugh.

"Okay calm down. Let me finish telling you about my honeymoon. After we returned to the boat that evening and had dinner, we slept all the way back to Miami. It was like being in a dream because as soon as we returned to Atlanta, Robert was back to work doing what he does best, working hard. However, while we were on our honeymoon Robert must have been on Viagra because I am worn out. I can really use the break."

"So, he wore your stuff out?" asked Sheila.

"Ladies, it would really take a day for me to tell you everything we did. I will finish by saying that the honeymoon was great. I would do it all again if I could."

"Well, it looks to me like we have ourselves another married woman. She has been taken off the market," said Cynthia.

"Yes, I have been taken off the market and given a little piece of my very own happiness. Robert and I have traveled two diverse roads but we found the way to each others heart."

"Well ladies, I have to get back to work. I had a great time. I can't wait to eat my rum cake Ann," said Melissa.

"Yea, she is right Ann. We need to be getting back to work too".

"All this talk about getting busy has made my 'thang' start to twitch. Now I need to call my baby and tell him to be ready tonight. I need to be spanked properly," said Sheila.

"Okay, Sheila, I heard you but I need to get some work accomplished today. So don't go getting your 'thang' spanked before you complete the project you said you would help me with."

All of us left the restaurant about the same time. I couldn't help but wonder what my Robert was doing. I believe I had gotten myself a little excited. I couldn't wait until I finished the day and returned home. But for now, I needed to turn my attention back to work and getting back to my routine.

During the course of lunch, no one said that Douglas was upset about my marriage so I guess I can face him with no regrets.

We soon arrived back at the office and you can't guess who was standing at the metal detector observing who and what was passing through. Yes, Mr. Douglas Brown was standing there in all his finesse.

"Well, hello Mrs. Robert Peterman. Come and give your friend Doug a hug. You got to know that I have missed you since you have been gone."

"Yeah, Right!"

"How long has it been? Three weeks I believe. Um, I am glad to see that you are ok."

"Okay, Douglas. I am happy to see you to. Is it possible for you to just be happy for me please?"

"For you Ann, I can always be happy. Although, I felt a little awkward standing here seeing you come through the door. You know that I am happy for you. I was just trying to be funny."

"Are you sure?"

"Yeah, I heard you were in the office so I just waited here to see if I could catch you coming back from lunch."

"I am glad Douglas. I really didn't want to wait all day to see you."

"I did look for you when I arrived this morning. I knew I had to run into you sooner or later."

"Can you come by the office later on Douglas so we can talk?"

"Okay, Mrs. Peterman."

As I started through the door, I saw the new girl Stephanie. She was with Cynthia and Sheila. I rushed passed so I could get to my office and start on a few new projects. I just needed to relax for a moment, collect my thoughts, and get back to the routine of work. I had a great vacation but it was tiresome. Robert and I had partied until we could no longer stand it. I needed another week just to recover from my honeymoon.

I had only been in the office five minutes when Mr. Green knocked on the door.

"Ann! Are you in there?"

"Yes, Mr. Green, I am reading my emails please come in."

"Come and give me a hug. I hope you had a beautiful wedding and honeymoon."

"Thanks Mr. Green. Everything was wonderful. Robert and I appreciated your gift."

"You are welcome, Ann. I just wanted to drop by and welcome you back. We will get together in a few days to work on the plans for the new collections department."

"Okay, Mr. Green."

Mr. Green left the office and closed the door behind him. I locked the door and got busy on the plans for the new collection department.

~ Chapter Fourteen ~

Confession

Good morning, Douglas, I am sorry about yesterday. I know we didn't get a chance to talk."

"I understand, Ann. I only wanted to say thanks for the letter. I am glad you let me know you were getting married. I guess that is one more thing I can scratch off my list."

"What do you mean?"

"Oh, nothing!"

"Come on we are friends you can tell me."

"Well, you know I have had a terrible time with women. I had hoped one day I would be worthy of your admiration. I know I have never told you but every since the day you started to work here, I have had a little crush on you. I have never said anything because I did not want it to ruin our friendship. Sometimes there are things that are better off not being said. I figured I had time to get to know you as a friend and hope you would see something that you liked in me."

"Douglas, I didn't know. I just thought that you and I were friends. I could tell you were a wonderful man and that is why I liked you so much. All of your wonderful compliments each day helped me through a very difficult transition period. Without you here at work each day, I would have never been able to get through my divorce. I know I never said anything, but you are the reason I was able to face my fears and start dating again."

"I appreciate your comments, Ann."

"Douglas, I must confess. There was this one time I thought you may have liked me more than as a friend but you never made a move to ask me out."

"Ann, I know. I didn't want to rush things and ruin our friendship."

"Well, Douglas, if I had really known you had a personal interest in me before I met Robert, things could have been different."

"I understand, Ann. If the opportunity ever presents itself again, I will take full advantage of it. Just remember if you ever need me I will always be here for you."

"Douglas, even if you find Mrs. Right?"

"Yes Ann, even if I find someone to fill the void in my life."

"So tell me Douglas, I hear you have been getting pretty friendly with a certain employee by the name of Stephanie."

"Well, she and I have developed a friendship. Stephanie is a very outgoing young lady that has a big challenge in front of her. I'm supposed to meet with her in a few minutes.

I am not even trying to get to home plate there. We have developed a friendship based on the fact that I am the operations manager and she is attempting to get close with the powers that be. I know that and I hope others see it also. She is much too young for a man my age. Besides, she has four kids. I have enough responsibility in my life. I don't need any 'baby daddy' drama."

"I know what you mean, Douglas."

"Ann, why don't you come with me to my office and I will introduce you to Stephanie."

"Okay, Douglas. I will be there in a few minutes."

As Douglas left my office, I saw Stephanie coming up the hallway. I quickly checked my hair and lipstick. Yes, I was taken off Douglas' list but I still had to look my best.

"Hi, Stephanie," I heard Douglas say from around the corner. I guessed that was my queue to come over and meet the new girl. I made my way over ensuring everything was in its proper place. As I approached Douglas' opened door, I saw that Stephanie had already sat in his chair. Douglas was leaning against his desk facing her. Their playful chemistry was apparent.

"Hello, Ann. Come in and meet Stephanie."

I saw her quickly look me over before I could even put my lips together to say it was nice to meet you.

“Hi, Stephanie, it is nice to meet you. My name is Ann Peterman.”

“Oh, I have heard a lot of good things about you. So, you are ‘number three’ now. I am ‘number two’ around here, since you just got married. I am just kidding, Ann. Everyone has been teasing me that Douglas gives you everything you want whenever you ask for it. You are the only one that doesn’t have to follow procedures. So I was told by Cynthia to have a little fun with you. Besides, you are married now. Did I say congratulations? I hope you had a great honeymoon.”

“Um, nice to meet you too, I said to myself.”

“I hope you are having a wonderful time having Douglas as your personal valet.”

“Ouch,” Douglas said.

Stephanie quickly grabbed me by the arms to reassure me.

”Ann I am only kidding. Everyone has told me nothing but great things about you.”

“Well ok. Thank you.” I said.

I didn’t know if she was teasing me or just trying to be funny.

“If that is the case, then I would like to welcome you to Bellsouth family. I know Douglas will take great care of you. He made my orientation be one I will forever be thankful for.

“I know. He is great,” Stephanie said looking back at Douglas with a big smile on her face.

“Ann, I have heard so much about your account receivables and the great job you and your staff are doing. I am looking forward to working with you. After you have been back for a while, I would love to sit down with you and discuss a possible partnership program.”

“I would love to, Stephanie”

“You see Ann, I told you she knows how to work with the movers and shakers of our organization.”

“You are right about that, Douglas,” I said.

I began to have thoughts of how self-aware I need to be. I better keep both eyes open at all times or she will work her way into my job.

I am just calling it like I see it. I am not jealous or anything. Sometime you have to call a female dog simply, a bitch!

I left Douglas' office with a lot of caution in my mind about the girl named Stephanie. I looked back to see if either of them were looking. No one was looking in my direction. I guess Stephanie had taken the number two spot in the office. I stood there for a moment just looking at them. Douglas was a great guy. I hope he knows what he is doing. Stephanie has the look of a woman that will take what she wants and discard the remainder. I turned around and went into my office. Douglas is a big boy and can take care of himself. I have my own life and my new husband needs much of my attention.

~ Chapter Fifteen ~

A Weekend in Miami

"Hello, Douglas," Stephanie said with the sweetest voice I had ever heard on the other end of a telephone.

"Hello Stephanie," I said with a smile catching the corner of my mouth.

"Douglas, I have purchased a tiny red bikini and I was wondering if you wanted to go to the beach with me in Miami."

"Did you say Miami?"

"Douglas, we both know Ann is married now and you deserve to have some fun."

"Well, Stephanie, what makes you think I want to go to Miami with you?"

"These two free airline tickets with free hotel accommodations I won on V-103 radio station."

"What?" I said excitedly.

"Yes, I won them last week. I was the tenth caller."

"So, why don't you take someone else?"

"I thought that you could use a small vacation. You need to relax and get over any worries you may have."

"Stephanie, now tell me why does everyone think I am so broken up over Ann's marriage. I am very happy for her. I was just caught off guard like everyone else. Marriage is a beautiful thing. I am very happy that Ann found Robert. If I wanted to pursue Ann, I would have months ago. I made a commitment to myself to stay single and that is what I am going to do. I value Ann's friendship and know that she values mine."

"Well, that is great Douglas. How would you like to value my friendship dressed up in a skimpy little two-piece?"

I thought long and hard for a minute while I sat silently in my chair. "Ok Stephanie, you got me for the weekend. When, where, and how do we get to Miami?"

"Just leave it all up to me. I have already made reservations at the Marriott. It is located on Miami Beach. We will depart at 3:00 pm on fight 1219 out of Atlanta on Friday. I will meet you at the airport. Once we get on the plane, I will fill you in on what else I have in store for us. The radio station gave me a few additional amenities."

"Ok, Stephanie, I'll call you tomorrow to confirm that everything is ok."

"Oh, everything is ready and I promise you that we will have a good time."

"Ok, I will call you tomorrow, Stephanie."

"Goodbye Douglas, I will see you tomorrow."

Well, I thought long and hard about the commitment I just made. If anyone found out that I spent the weekend in Miami with Stephanie, I would have a lot of explaining to do. What the heck? I needed a good weekend vacation. Maybe a couple of days with Stephanie would make me more relaxed. I have been feeling a little tense lately.

The next day, I called Stephanie on my cell phone while driving to the airport. The time was about 12:00 noon. I was a little excited to hear her voice. She stated she was almost there. It would be a good trip for two friends. As I approached the airport exit off I-285, I found myself full of tiny little butterflies. I started to imagine how it would be if it were Ann and I going on this trip instead of Stephanie. I smiled at the thought and started the drive to the park and fly.

I soon arrived at the airport and there stood Stephanie with her hair down, dressed in a white top and an orange pair of shorts that resembled a skirt. She looked as beautiful as any woman I had ever seen. I had never really looked at her with any real interest before. I had been so consumed with admiring Ann that other women did not catch my eye the same way.

"Hi, Douglas," how was the drive to the Airport?"

"Great!"

She gave me a little hug and a big kiss on the lips.

"I hope you are ready for a weekend of fun and games. I have packed light so we can go shopping in Miami and tour the city. You will see. We will have a great time.

"Ok, Stephanie, lets get on the plane first."

Stephanie was full of energy. We checked our bags at the Sky Cap (outside counter) and headed for the AirTran terminal. As we arrived at the terminal, Stephanie began to hold my arm as if we were a couple. She kept looking into my eyes as if she wanted to eat me up. At one point, I leaned closer to her to hear what she was saying and found my ear being nibbled on. Of course, I was in no position to object to her advances. She was a fine specimen of a woman. I had agreed to accompany her on this trip without considering her motives.

After we boarded, I found myself alone with Stephanie in the rear section of the plane. Everything seemed to be perfect. Stephanie was becoming friendlier than I had imagined she would be.

"Well, Douglas, I told you I had a surprise for you."

"What is my surprise?" I asked.

"I used to be an airline stewardess. I have several of my friends on this flight. This will be a weekend you will never forget. As soon as we get airborne, I will give you your first surprise."

"First surprise," I said in a low voice. I didn't think it was possible but the beat of my heart started to increase. I guess I was beginning to get more excited about what was going to happen next.

"Yes, your first surprise. I will give it to you as soon as the in-flight movie starts."

I really didn't have a clue about what the surprise could be. However, it wasn't long before I found out.

"Hello, Stephanie," said a fight attendant handing her a hot towel.

"Hello, Myra. Is everything set?"

"Yes," everything is just like you requested."

Little did I know we were on a double deck airbus that would eventually fly out of Miami to Brazil. The upstairs level seated primarily first class passengers. All the coach seats were reserved for passengers that would fly to Miami. The airbus had a small compartment in the rear of the upstairs section for the crew to sleep during international flights. Stephanie and I were escorted by Myra upstairs. After we were seated, she commenced giving me my first gift.

"Just lay back and relax I will take care of everything from here, Douglas."

The towel Myra gave Stephanie was still hot. I could feel the heat penetrate my skin. Slowly, she moved the towel down my face until every inch was clean. I sat there totally relaxed. I really didn't expect her to take care of me. She laid the towel down and massaged my neck. She took a bottle of massage oil out of her carry on bag. Her hands were warm and soft. I relaxed as she massaged my entire body. I was filled with total excitement as I enjoyed having my body manipulated at thirty thousand feet. It was an unexpected pleasure.

"How did you like your first surprise Douglas?"

"I enjoyed it very much. It was an unexpected pleasure."

"Well, you haven't seen anything yet."

My heart started beating faster like I had just run a marathon.

"Well, take this little pill and I will be back in a minute."

"What is it?" I asked.

"Trust me. It is something that will help you prevail in your next quest. It will help you stay focus during the remainder of this flight. Besides, your first surprise is not complete."

I didn't waste any time swallowing the small pill. I was the student and she definitely knew how to instruct, thirty thousand feet in the air, I received a great massage. It was a surprise I never thought I would get and to top it off, I was about to receive the second half of the surprise.

Well, it didn't take long for the little pill to start working its magic. I could feel my blood flowing through my veins. The beat of my heart continued to increase. These were clear signs that I was about to have muscles growing all over me. Stephanie had perfect timing.

"Are you ok, Douglas?"

"Sure! I am fine." I was totally blown away by your gift.

"I could tell you needed a little relaxing. I just thought that since we were going on this trip together that we might as well have some excitement and a lot of fun."

"Well, let the fun begin," I said.

"How is everything down there?"

"Great!"

"Come to me then."

Oh boy, I thought as she put her lips on my lips. They were soft and silky. She moved them up and down each side of mine. The stimulation caused me to pull back. I felt her hands touch my shoulder pulling me closer. My heartbeat increased with every stroke of her hands and with every kiss. I found myself a willing participant. She sat me down on the seat and we disappeared into the clouds. The only thing I remember is that she had a body that the Greek goddess Aphrodite must have carved herself. Stephanie had the ability to expose a man's inner desires. I must confess, it was an honor to receive the delight of my first complete surprise. As we reached the climax of our journey, I fell back into the chair trying to absorb what had happened.

"Now, Douglas, how did you like your complete surprise?"

"I have to admit it was great! I never thought that I could re-live my youth again and be free spirited on an airplane."

"You just wait until we get to Miami I am going to give you a weekend to remember."

After another quick massage session that lasted about thirty minutes, I was almost exhausted. I went to the lavatory to wash my face. After I had finished, I saw Myra standing next to the beverage stand with a big smile on her face.

"Hello again, Douglas, I hope your flight is everything you hoped it would be."

"It is. Thank you very much, Myra."

"Stephanie had asked that I make sure you two had complete privacy."

"I really appreciate your assistance."

"Where is Stephanie?"

"She went to the lavatory up front."

"Come here and let me show you something."

I went inside a small compartment near the beverage stand. Myra closed the door behind her and locked it. She put the key in her blouse.

"Wow," I said another surprise.

Stephanie and I didn't have a serious relationship. I figured that Myra was part of the surprise that Stephanie had planned. Myra pulled the curtain closed and I didn't waste any time. I took off my shirt ready to lie down and receive another massage. Her hands were strong. Her legs pressed against my back as she saddled me slowly moving her hands back and forth keeping contact with each of my muscles. The deeper her finger went the more relaxed I became. Finally, she pushed one last time into my lower back and I heard it pop. I felt her pushing down as my leg lodged against her pelvis. She began to speak softly.

"Was that good for you, Douglas?"

I looked back at Myra to make sure she was not massaging anything else. We stayed there for a minute while I enjoyed the last stroke of her hands on my lower back. I put on my shirt leaving Myra in her compartment. After ten minutes or so, I finally made it back to where I had last seen Stephanie. She was sitting in one of the regular seats watching the in-flight movie. As I sat in the seat beside her, she asked what took me so long. I quickly realized that the massage I received from Myra was not part of any surprise Stephanie had planned.

"Oh, I had to let go a major one. I just took my time and rested while I was in the lavatory."

"Are you ready for your second surprise?"

"No, no we need to get our feet back on the ground."

"Ok, Douglas, don't you go getting tired on me."

"Don't worry, I won't."

"I hope not. I have a wonderful weekend planned for us."

The plane soon landed at the Miami International Airport. Guess who stood at the front door to say goodbye. Yes, Myra was standing there waving her pretty head off. As a matter of fact, she had forgotten to put her uniform back on correctly. I just smiled and exited the plane with Stephanie.

It was not long after we exited the plane and retrieved our luggage, that we caught the shuttle to the Marriott hotel. After we checked in to our amazing suite, we took a shower and continued where we left off on the plane. It was simply incredible. I felt like a twenty year old again. I was so excited, that I arrived a little quicker than normal. Stephanie fully understood. We got dress and caught the city train to South Beach. It was a great way to get around. We didn't have much time to see everything because we had to catch an 11:00 a.m. flight out on Sunday morning.

"So, Douglas, how do you like Miami?"

"I must admit, Stephanie, it is more than what I expected."

Stephanie held my hand and treated me like I was her mate. She made me feel very relaxed. She had never shown affection like this at work. She was very cordial and sometimes playful.

"Oh, Douglas, I just want to forget about all my worries this weekend. My ex-husband has been a royal pain. I needed this weekend to relax with someone I can trust and who didn't have complications. I know you may have been overwhelmed by the affection and sex. I needed it just as bad as you may have. I am not looking for a relationship. I just need your close companionship this weekend."

"I understand fully. I really needed to let my hair down too. So what ever you want to do this weekend will be our little secret."

"It's a deal."

As the train stopped, we exited at the Marina of South Beach. There were fifty different restaurants and fast food stands to chose from. The building was as big as a football field. There were stores and clothing outlets on each of the three levels. The look in

Stephanie's eyes told me she had found her personal smorgasbord. She was so excited; however, I needed to replenish my energy level with a big juicy steak and a loaded baked potato.

We chose a steak and salad restaurant called Chops. We were given a table with a beautiful view of the yachting marina. The setting was simply enchanting.

"So, what do you want to do after we eat?"

"Douglas I would like to take a long walk on the beach and be held in your arms for a while. I need a little comforting. Then after that I want to shop until I drop."

"Well, I think I can handle that."

After we finished our meal, we did just that. It was great. I had never been on a beach in Florida before. It was like I had been sent to paradise. I didn't even think of Ann and my life back in Atlanta. This weekend was just what I needed to forget all the ladies I had ever met. If paradise was anything like Miami, I was going to live right here.

"Come on Douglas, it is time to go shopping."

"Ok, lets' have some fun."

"I need something to sleep in. I forgot to pack my night gown."

"I like to sleep in my personal body amour. That way I can always be ready for battle."

"I understand, Douglas. I just like the feel of something soft against my skin."

"How do you like this black negligee, Stephanie?"

"Um, that looks interesting. Ok, I will take that for you and this T-Shirt to wear around the room. Now, I need to buy a pair of shorts and top to wear on the beach tomorrow. This will do fine. What do you think Douglas?"

"I like it. I can't wait to see you wear it."

"Ok, Douglas, this is great. I need to go back to the hotel and drop these things off. I want to get ready for a night of dancing and fun."

We returned to the hotel and took a quick shower. I did not get in the shower with Stephanie this time. I needed a break just in case she wanted to go at it later on. I had already given a grand performance and that was a record for me. When Stephanie started to get dressed,

I went into the shower and relaxed. There was a small tiled bench to sit on. I just sat there and allowed the water to hit my body. It was so relaxing. I didn't realize how much I needed this vacation. I don't know if I could ever repay Stephanie for this weekend, but I was going to be the best companion she could ever ask for.

"Douglas, have you finished, we need to get to the club before ten."

"I am coming. I will be right out."

I turned the water off and dried off. There stood Stephanie in all her glory. She pulled a black dress over her head. It fitted perfectly showing off each curve of her body. I became excited again but I knew I would never make it to the club if I tried to get under that dress she was wearing. I quickly put on my charcoal gray slacks, my black body shirt, and my gold chain with a cross. We were a pair.

"Douglas, don't forget to knock the dust off those shoes. I saw a shoe shine kit in the bathroom."

I quickly shined my shoes and off we went hand in hand having the time of our lives. We must have kissed twenty times during that short ride to South Beach. When we arrived, Stephanie took me to Club Apocalypse. It was there I would receive my second surprise.

"Are you ready, Douglas?"

"Am I ready for what?"

"Well, we have a VIP booth all to ourselves."

"Dam girl! Did V-103 do this?"

"No, I know the manager from when I worked as a stewardess. He is a good friend of mine. He told me many years ago if I ever came back to Miami to just let him know. So we can dance here or down on the floor."

"So who provided the champagne?"

"A gift from an old friend and there he is."

Stephanie waved at a Hispanic gentleman entertaining four other guests.

"I am sure he will come by later on. I talked to him before we flew down. He is just a great friend. I told you that you would enjoy this trip."

"I am having the time of my life."

Stephanie reached into her purse and gave me two aspirins and another small pill.

"Take the aspirin now, but don't take the pill until we have our last dance. I want you to be ready when we get back to the hotel."

"I will be ready. That little outfit you have on will do the trick."

"I was hoping you would say that."

Needless to say Stephanie and I danced the night away. We were all over the club having fun. We left around two o'clock in the morning. The manager had one of the drivers take us back to the hotel.

I hardly remember much about Friday night. We drank a lot of champagne. It was a miracle we made it back at all. Saturday morning around eleven o'clock, I took a quick shower and put on my clothes. I made fresh coffee and took it out on the balcony. Stephanie was sleeping like a baby. Although I was having the time of my life, I thought about how nice it would have been to be with Ann. I thought of what she was doing with her new husband, Robert. I guess as long as she was happy I could love her forever as a friend.

"Well, there you are, Douglas!"

"Yes, here I am. I didn't want to wake you. You looked so beautiful sleeping."

"Douglas, I had a great time last night."

"I did too Stephanie. Your friend was very nice."

"Who, Carlos?

"Yes, Carlos. He seems to be a great guy. He told me to tell you to call him today."

"Douglas, I don't remember talking to him last night."

"I know you had a great time drinking champagne all night. He had one of his drivers bring us back to the hotel."

"That was nice of him. I am going to take a shower and put on the hot outfit I purchased yesterday."

"Okay, I will be in after you take a shower."

I went back to enjoying the morning breeze as I watched the sun rise high in the Marina. It was a beautiful Saturday morning. I needed to buy a hat to protect me from the Miami heat. The weather was great but the sun got a little hot at times if you were not on the beach. The cool breeze blowing on shore kept the beach goers cool during the day.

"I am ready, Douglas," said Stephanie sounding pretty excited.

Well, here I go again. I hope I can keep up with this gift of nature. Off we went back to South Beach to enjoy a day in the sun and eat brunch at a little coffee shop we had seen the day before. They served the best bagels with a splendid variety of cream cheeses.

When we arrived at the shop, we were given a table facing the marina. Stephanie ordered a cinnamon bagel topped with fresh strawberries. I had a butter-fried bagel topped with apple jelly. It was delicious. Just as we finished off the bagels, a boat was pulling up into the marina.

"It is time to go, Douglas."

"It is time to go where, Stephanie?"

"Well, it is time for your third and final surprise."

What in the world could be next?

"Okay, I agreed to go along with the plan for the weekend. I am ready to get busy." She led me out to the pier and we got on this one hundred foot yacht. It was magnificent. The boat belonged to Carlos. He allowed us to use it for the day. With all the contacts Stephanie had, I was beginning to wonder why she didn't move to Miami. This was a huge favor from Carlos. I don't have friends like him. Hell, I don't know of anyone else who has friends like him. I soon got over the shock of my third surprise and began to enjoy being on the yacht.

"Come on, Douglas, we can lay here on the sun bed."

"What sun bed! I have never heard of a sun bed before."

"Yes, everyone who has a yacht has a sun bed. You see, two people can lie on it. Come hold me for a little while."

We laid there enjoying the sun as the captain of the boat took us for a ride around the huge marina. There was a cover over the bed that shielded the sun's harmful rays. It was the life of the rich and famous. We spent the day drinking wine coolers. We didn't want to get toasted while we were out on the water. Stephanie and I talked about how she had met Carlos years ago while she was an airline stewardess and how her first husband was a close friend of Carlos. She said that after the breakup she and Carlos remained friends. They were never involved. Carlos was just a true friend.

After three hours, we soon finished our tour of the marina and returned to the pier. We exited the boat and took a long walk on the beach. We talked about her whole life. It was quite amazing that she was still so upbeat about everything. We promised each other to remain friends no matter what happened after we returned back to Atlanta.

After the walk on the beach Stephanie had one last surprise. We returned to the hotel at about 8:00 p.m. We walked through the door and our dinner was waiting for us. She had planned everything to the letter. Hell, I had begun to wish I could afford her and all her kids. But I knew it would have been too much drama for me. We washed our hands and dug in.

"How is your steak?" Stephanie asked.

"It is almost as delicious as you."

"Well, we will see about that. You got off easy last night. But tonight you must take me to that place that no other woman has gone before."

"Where is that?" I asked with a smile on my face.

"You know, to the edge of heaven."

"Oh, oh I believe I can grant you that wish."

We finished off our meal and got dressed for the evening. I didn't think it was possible. Stephanie had a red evening dress that was quite revealing.

"Turn on the CD player, Douglas. I want to dance with you here in the room tonight."

I opened the entertainment console to see a CD player and all sorts of jazz CD's. For a minute, I thought I had entered a movie. I put in a CD she requested and went into the bathroom to look for the little pill Stephanie had given me the night before. I quickly swallowed it along with a glass of water. I returned to find Stephanie on the balcony. She was as beautiful as each of the stars in the sky. I took her in my arms and danced the evening away. We only paused to take in a few two minute kisses. After a couple of hours of dancing, we moved into the bedroom. We started to kiss as we made our own music.

"Take me tonight, Douglas, for tomorrow I must return to my life and to my world. I need you to make this night last for all eternity. You have been a great friend to me since I moved to Atlanta. Tonight I want to thank you for your friendship and love. Love me slowly. Make me remember this night forever."

With that request, Stephanie and I spent the night among the stars. When the night was over, the stars seem to explode in the night sky. We kissed one last time and slept until morning.

Sunday morning I laid in bed watching Stephanie sleep. She was so at peace with herself. In a few hours, we would get on the plane and return to Atlanta as if nothing happened. I gently rubbed her face awaking her.

I kissed her on the lips and said, "Wake up sleepy head."

"Douglas, is it time?"

"Yes, my good friend it is time to leave paradise and return to Atlanta."

She pulled me close. "Thanks Douglas for being a good friend. You are the best friend any women could have. I really needed you with me this weekend. You don't have to worry. I won't act like we are a couple when we get back to Atlanta. As a matter of fact, I am returning to California in a few months. My kids need to be near their father. I have to do what is best for them. I needed to enjoy freedom one last time before I return to California and all the drama of parenthood and ex-husbands. You helped me to enjoy that freedom."

Stephanie kissed me and we made love one last time. At 9:00 a.m. we got dressed and signed out of the hotel on our way to the airport. We caught our flight at 11:00 a.m. and flew back to Atlanta. We were on a regular flight this time, sitting in regular chairs. We had a regular movie. All the way there, I smiled to myself. I kept squeezing Stephanie's hand. I had been given the opportunity to have my cake and eat it to. Stephanie tried to smile and let me know everything would be all right. I felt a little sad, but I knew she would have the weekend we spent in Miami to remember for the rest of her life.

~ Chapter Sixteen ~

Ann and Robert

"Good morning, Robert."

"Good morning, my love!"

"Robert, what time will you be home this evening?"

"I can't be certain my love. You know how the sales business is. I have several appointments this afternoon. Can we meet for lunch at eleven today? I have been working on a big sales presentation to present to Coca-Cola. If I can land their advertising contract, we will be set for a while."

"I understand, Robert. I just wanted to know if I had to make dinner tonight."

"No, don't worry about me. I will eat with my client or pick something up on the way home."

"Ok, Robert. Good luck."

"I'll see you at 11:00 a.m. for lunch."

As soon as Robert left, I got ready to go to work. I see everything his mother told me was true. I really don't mind because he takes care of business at home. On the way to work, I thought about my happiness and how lucky I was to be married to Robert. We have a beautiful home, two nice cars and two great jobs. Being married is a full time job in itself. I need to be sensitive to Robert's work ethics. I know I have a crazy work schedule myself.

I had no sooner arrived at work, when I was greeted by Sheila.

"Hello, Ann, I hope you had a great weekend."

"I did, and you?"

"Girl, it was the bomb!"

"It is great to have everything back to normal," I said as I continued to my office.

"Girl, you are right about that. I hope you have a great day Ann."

"I hope you have a great day too Sheila."

I finally made it to my office. I put by purse down and went to the break room to pour a cup of coffee. There was Mr. Douglas Brown sitting at his desk with none other than Stephanie tied to his hip. I knocked on the door to say good morning.

"Good morning, Douglas and Stephanie how are the both of you?"

"Oh, hi, Ann," Douglas said rising from his seat like he was startled.

"Hi, number three," Stephanie said with her usual smile.

I wanted to kick her number three ass but I just smiled and went on my way.

I went into the break room and poured me a cup of coffee, and returned to my desk. As I was returning to my office, I noticed Flora was standing next to my door waiting for me.

"Ann, we have a meeting at 10:00 a.m. this morning. We need to discuss the management of the new collections department."

"Flora, I have a small problem. I need to meet my husband at 11:00 a.m. for lunch. Do you think we will be finish by then?"

"I don't know. We can change the time to later on in the day if you like, Ann."

"That would be great."

Flora left my office and I started to work on the organization structure for the new department. With all the activities in the past month, I didn't have time to get much done. Many of the activities are routine. However, I needed to plan the grand opening and arrange for a guest speaker for the opening ceremony. There was a sudden knock at my door.

"Who is it, now?"

"It's Sheila. I know you are trying to get work done, but you really need to open your door."

"Ok, I am coming."

Little did I know Sheila was standing outside of my door with a vase of twenty-four yellow roses?

"Are those for me Sheila?" I asked.

I was totally surprised by their arrival. Now who would send me roses?

"Thanks Sheila."

"Who are they from, Sheila asked?"

"I don't know," I said reluctantly. I closed the door and took the roses into my office. I looked for a note and found one hidden in the middle of the roses. There was a small card that listed the name of the flower shop. On it was a small encryption that read, "To the love of my life." There was no signature or initials. It didn't matter who sent them. I was happy to receive them. I needed this small gift to lift my spirits and get me focused on the task at hand.

I got back to work. I made a quick agenda for the new department's opening ceremonies and called my trusted contact, Jan Wilson, senior marketing director for Bellsouth. She agreed to be the guest speaker. Now everything was set for my meeting with Flora. She had the responsibility to make sure everything was coordinated down to the letter. I didn't want to let her down or get my butt chewed off in the process. No matter what anyone thought of Flora and her love life, she was a good friend and a great co-worker. If she is in charge of a project, you can bet it would be done right.

As I was making final preparations for my departure to meet Robert for lunch, Douglas stuck his head in the door to see if I had any lunch plans.

"I'm sorry, Douglas. I am meeting Robert for lunch."

"Douglas, do you know that this is the first time you have asked me to lunch?"

"Yes, I know. Well, you have been married for over a year now. I just thought that it would be okay for two co-workers to sit down and have a quiet lunch."

"Well, how about a rain check?"

"A rain check will be fine. I really like you as a friend and I don't see why we can't be friends even though you are married. You know if you were my wife, I would send you flowers at least once a week."

"What? Oh you mean the flowers."

"Yeah, they are more beautiful than when I saw them in the flower shop."

"What do you mean, Douglas?"

"Those flowers, I sent them to you. This week marks your third year with Bellsouth's southeastern location. I just wanted to say congratulations on becoming vested in the retirement system."

"But the card reads, 'To the love of my life'."

"What? They must have gotten the cards mixed up. I sent roses to my mother too. It is a note I always send her. We use to joke all the time that I would grow up and find a wife and not love her anymore. So I always include a card saying 'to the love of my life.' I am sorry about the mix up. I know you would have to answer questions from Robert if you had told him thank you for the flowers."

"There is no problem Douglas. I would not have mentioned it unless he brought it up. I really appreciate your thoughtfulness. You have really made my employment here easy. Thanks for the flowers and thanks for being you."

I gave Douglas a hug and kissed him on the face. He was indeed a good friend. Time really goes by quickly. I was late meeting Robert at Ruby's Tuesdays. He was sitting in our favorite booth when I arrived.

"Hello, my love," he said standing up to greet me.

"Hello, Robert. I am sorry I am running a little late."

"I completely understand' Ann. I am in the business of being too early or being just a little bit late."

"So, what are you having?"

"I ordered my usual, a Caesar salmon salad. I took the liberty of ordering you a garden salad with salmon."

"That will be just fine. So tell me Robert how is your briefing coming along."

"I have completed it. I am ready to brief the Coke reps at three today. It will be a long meeting and I am prepared to answer every question that they could possible have."

"Great! I wish you good-luck."

"Good luck! Ann, I have them in the bag. I am just waiting to receive that big bonus check."

"I know. I have a meeting as soon as I get back myself. So I am going to have to hurry up so I can get back on time."

"I understand Ann; I really enjoy the opportunities we have to sit down for a quiet meal. I know my schedule is hectic. I will try to minimize all unnecessary meetings I can."

"Thank you so much, Robert. I really do love you."

"I know Ann."

With that being said, Robert and I finished off our salads and departed. I had a meeting with Flora that I could not put off another day. On the way back to the office, I thought of what Robert's mother had told me concerning Robert's dedication to his work. I fully understand and have accepted the fact that at times Robert and I will be like two ships at sea passing in the night. At times, work will take a toll on the both of us. I just need to be at home for him when he needs me to be.

Later that night, I waited for Robert to come home. It was after 9:00 p.m. and I hadn't heard from him. I called his cell phone to see if he was ok. Robert answered the phone speaking in a low voice.

"Is everything okay, Robert?" I asked.

"Yes, Ann, I am on my way home now. We had a little celebration after the Coke deal went through. I got the contract."

"That is great sweetheart. I will see you when you come home."

I went fast asleep after my conversation with Robert. I did not know what time he got home. He was lying beside me when I awoke the next morning.

~ Chapter Seventeen ~

Stephanie's Departure

The day had finally come. My good buddy Stephanie was about to complete her last day at work. Next week she would pack up her house and get ready for her return trip to California. There were only a handful of us who knew. Stephanie and I had become good friends and we had sealed that friendship with a weekend that I know we will never forget. I was sad to see her go. We were like two teenagers having fun in high school. She provided me with the strength to let my feelings be known. I had finally expressed my true feelings to Ann. Without Stephanie, I don't think I would have ever been able to tell Ann how much she really means to me as a friend. I owe Stephanie a lot. Life is funny sometimes. It seems that I would have fallen in love with Stephanie after what the both of us experienced together. I guess love is not based solely on what you may experience with a person, but how you see that person with your heart. I will truly miss Stephanie, but I know I would not be able to deal with the 'baby daddy drama' that she has in her life.

"Let's go Douglas," Tony shouted as he passed my door. We are going to be late for Stephanie's going away luncheon."

"What do you mean, Tony?"

"Well, I know Stephanie didn't want anyone to make a big scene over her leaving so I arranged with Cynthia to bring her to Ruby's Tuesday so her close friends could say good-bye."

"Well, now. That is a surprise. I thought she told Cynthia that she did not want to have a farewell luncheon. Okay. I'll be right there."

I quickly grabbed my coat and hurried out the office. Stephanie was getting into Cynthia's car when I was pulling out of the parking lot.

When I arrived at Ruby Tuesday's I saw Tony, Tonya, and Melissa going into the restaurant.

I quickly parked and went into the restaurant before Stephanie and Cynthia arrived.

"So what is going on Tony?"

"Well, we knew that Stephanie didn't want to have a big send off so we got with Cynthia and coordinated this small luncheon for her."

"I am glad you did. She will really be happy to see that her fellow co-workers appreciated her."

At the end of my sentence, Stephanie and Cynthia walked into the restaurant where we were sitting.

"Surprise Stephanie we love you!" shouted Tonya and Melissa.

Tony and I could hardly get a word out. The look in Stephanie's eyes said it all. She was so happy that her closest friends came out to have lunch with her.

"Cynthia, this is a surprise. I didn't imagine that all of you would be here."

"Well, it is our way of saying that we enjoyed working with you and that we will miss you Stephanie," said Tony.

"I will miss all of you to. I need to get back to California so my kids can be around their father. It was great being here and I am glad to have been a part of the yellow pages department for Bellsouth. I will carry the friendships and fun memories I have of all of you. Thank you so much. I really appreciate this luncheon."

Tears began to form in Stephanie's eyes as Cynthia put her arms around her. I smiled knowing that she would be all right. She will always have the weekend we spent in Miami to remember me by. I am not sad that she is leaving because I understand how she feels about her kids and their needs. I would never let my own wishes or desires come before the needs of my children. Stephanie is a great mother and she will be successful no matter where she lives. She also has a great mom helping her raise her kids.

"Ok, since we have all ordered, I would like to say a few words," said Tony. Stephanie, as you know, I have enjoyed your friendship very much. We have had an opportunity to talk about a lot of things. I will miss you a lot. I have enjoyed seeing your smiling face and observing your wonderful walk up the hallway to Douglas' office."

Everyone let out a low laugh. Tony continued to talk.

"I will most of all miss the smile on your face and the gleam you keep in your eyes that says you are beautiful and one of God's wonderful spirits he has placed upon the earth."

"Thank you, Tony, I will miss you to."

"Well Douglas it is your turn," said Cynthia.

"Ok, Ok, let me see. Where do I start? I know you asked us not to give you a big send off. I agreed to comply with your wishes. I didn't know about this luncheon until Tony told me when he was leaving out of the door. I am glad that we were able to come together and say farewell. It is a privileged opportunity to have met you. It is a pleasure to have served you. It is my heart that is hurting knowing that you are leaving. I regret that I want see you each morning when I come to work. A great poet once wrote a letter to a friend to tell her that he understood the reason why she had the life she had. He wanted her to know that if he could take the pain away, he would. The poem reads:

If you told me to cry just one tear so your pain would leave from inside,

I would spend one day crying just for you.

If one kiss would make your pain go away, I would kiss you forever and a day.

If you needed happiness to live, all my love I would give.

My heart would drain all the sadness from inside of you.

If you needed the blood in my veins,

I would extend my arms to the heavens so it could rain.

My very essence would be yours so you can live.

If you needed me to die, the whole world would watch and cry.

For my life I would offer up to you.

If our friendship is to last, we must never forget our past.

Remember I will always be here just for you.

"That was so beautiful," Cynthia said. "I hope when I leave you recite a poem at my luncheon."

"I will if I have the opportunity. Today is Stephanie's day and I am glad that I was told about the luncheon."

Stephanie came over to me and thanked me personally for the poem. She kissed me on the lips.

"Thank you so much Douglas. I will miss you most. You have indeed been a close friend. I will miss all of you. Thanks for the lunch. With that speech, Stephanie left out the restaurant crying. Cynthia left behind her. We all understood now why Stephanie did not want a farewell luncheon. She gets very emotional. I smiled to myself because I knew the real reason why Stephanie was leaving. I also had a gift from her that no one could take away.

"Well, I guess it is time to go back to work," said Tony.

"I guess so," said Tonya and Melissa.

"Why don't the three of you go ahead? I will take care of the bill." They all left. I just sat there for a while thinking about how much I would miss Stephanie and the good time she and I shared in Miami.

~ Chapter Eighteen ~

Grand Opening of the New Collection Department

Good morning, Flora."

"Good morning, Ann."

"Have you seen Tonya and Tony?"

"No, Flora, I haven't."

"I bet that boy is up to no good."

"What do you mean?"

"You didn't here about him and Tonya?"

"No I didn't, Flora."

"It was when we moved to the new office three years ago. Douglas caught Tony and Tonya getting it on in my new office."

"They were in your new office?"

"Yeah, I bet that boy and Tonya are somewhere in this building spreading their love juices everywhere."

"I hope not Flora. It is almost time for people to start arriving. So tell me Flora, is Mr. Tuesday coming."

"Who is Mr. Tuesday, Ann?"

"You know, a certain director of Sam's on Stone Mountain Freeway."

"Are you talking about Anthony?"

"Yes," I said.

"Girl, he better attend. All the cookies I have thrown his way. He better come here to support us."

"Flora, did you call me?" said Tony.

"Boy, where is Tonya?"

"I believe I saw her go into the restroom."

"The both of you better get cleaned up and get out front. People will start arriving any minute now. And another thing; zip up your fly before your horse gets out and start riding Tonya again."

"Yes, Flora."

"Girl you are tough when you want to be," I said.

"Yeah! Every now and then you have to get tough with these kids. If you are too nice, they will take that as a weakness."

"I know what you mean Flora."

"Well, everything seems to be on schedule. Are you ready to move outside to the podium?"

"Yes Ann, I hope Douglas got everything connected up properly. He has been a little of out of it since Stephanie left. I guess you have moved back up to the number two spot."

"Actually, I never moved out of the number two spot. Douglas was a little confused because Stephanie threw a little nookie his way. It was like you and Mr. Tuesday."

"Girl I don't know what to say about that man. Last night he dropped by the house for a quickie. I had been drinking a little wine. He jumped through the door and kissed his way back to my bedroom. I had to put him on hold because I needed to get mine. I made him get down on all fours while I sat on the bed. I took my riding paddle and spanked him while he had dinner."

"Not while he had dinner?"

"Yes, girl. He had dinner right in my bedroom. The main course was Flora on satin sheets. You can bet he was full when he finished. I finally gave him his feel and then he ran back home to his wife."

"Flora, you deserve better than that."

"I know, but a girl got to do what a girl got to do."

"Look, the guess speaker just arrived. Flora, we better get out there and help the director and Douglas get everything in place."

Everything was perfect for the opening of the new department. Flora and I had done a great job. The director was well pleased with the ceremony and presentation of guests. Robert's company had donated a lot of the food and door prizes since Bellsouth was one of their clients. I was looking forward to possibly having Robert eat dinner in our bedroom later on that night. However, I had to work late and I didn't know exactly what time Robert would be coming home."

"Ann, come in here. I want to show you something."

"What is it, Flora?"

"I would like to introduce you to Anthony Woodworth."

"How are you sir, I have heard a lot about you."

"I am fine. How are you and Douglas?"

"Excuse me!"

"No, Anthony, she did not marry Douglas. Ann's husband is named Robert."

"Please forgive me, Ann. It has been along time since I received a current briefing." But I would like to congratulate you on your marriage and I hope all is well."

"Thank you very much, Mr. Tuesday. Oh, I mean Mr. Woodworth."

Flora quickly nudged me in the side. "Well, I have to go. It was nice meeting you Mr. Woodworth."

"Goodbye Ann," I heard the both of them say as I hurried out of the office before I bursted into laughter. I knew Flora would get me for the mistake I made. But it was funny calling him Mr. Woodworth when we all called him Mr. Tuesday behind his back. Just then, I my phone rang. It was Robert.

"Hello sweetheart."

"Hi Robert," I said in a soft sexy voice.

"Baby I am on my way home. What time will you get off work?"

"I am almost finished here. I will be home in an hour."

"That is great. I will be there waiting on you."

"Okay, Robert, I will see you soon."

I ran back to my office to get my purse. I was getting excited minute by minute. As soon as I unlocked the door, I saw the director and Douglas coming up the hallway. I knew I was going to be held up. There was no way to escape.

"Hello, Ann. The ceremony was great. You and Flora really did a great job."

"Thank you very much, Mr. Green."

"Yes, Ann. I was really impressed with everything."

"Well, thank you Douglas, but we could not have pulled everything off without your great operational support."

"Thanks, Ann, but this is Flora and your hour to shine."

"Once again, thanks for the great job."

"Thank you, Mr. Green."

Douglas just smiled at me like he always does. He was with the number one person in the office now. He really knew the proper relationship that an employee needed to have with his boss. No one had a higher priority than Mr. Green, not even Stephanie or me.

~ Chapter Nineteen ~

Robert's Heart Attack

When I arrived home, Robert was dressed in his smoking jacket and a pair of black silk boxers. He was sipping on a glass of Hennessey and reading the business section of the paper. There was a slow jazz song in the background that sounded like Herbie Hancock.

"Oh, hi baby, I didn't here you come in."

'That's alright my love I was admiring you relaxing."

"Come here and give me a kiss."

I didn't wait. I jumped into his arms giving him all the love I had. We kissed for a good five minutes.

"Wait a minute baby. Let me go and freshen up," I said catching my breath.

"Okay my love. I will be here waiting on you."

I ran into the bedroom pulling off my clothes on my way to the shower. I wanted to make sure that everything was ready for Robert. I selected Robert's favorite perfume and put a little in all my kissable places. Lastly, I put on the black satin negligee Robert had given me for my birthday.

I cut the lights down low in the bedroom and went into the den. Robert was waiting for me. I walked up to him putting his face in my hands. He slowly took me into his arms. He kissed me softly. His hands moved up and down my body. I lay there enjoying the moment while he continued to kiss me. I felt the love I had for him build as passion ran deep within me. His body felt firm as he lay next to me. We were like shooting stars ready to descend into the night. I was filled with his love. He was the perfect man. We both rode into the night as time seemed to have no meaning. Finally, we descended back to earth leaving the stars to explore the universe. Robert called my name in a low voice letting me know that he could feel my love within me. As I lay next to Robert, I could feel his heart beating rapidly. His breathing was fast and irregular. I helped roll him over on the couch as I got up to shower.

"That was great Ann," Robert said.

I kissed him on the lips and went into the bathroom. I started the shower and waited for Robert to join me. Robert normally followed me into the bathroom. I called for him, but he did not answer. I finished washing up and dried my body. As I walked back into the den I found Robert on the floor with his hand over his heart. I shook him several times trying to get him to wake up. I checked his pulse and could not feel anything. I checked his heart and felt a light beat. Robert's body was turning cold. I ran to the hallway closet. I and got a blanket to put on him. He was barely breathing. I called 911 and told the operator what had happened. They dispatched an ambulance to my location. I quickly put Roberts's pants on. Ten minutes later, the ambulance arrived. I was dressed in my nightgown and robe. The paramedic quickly assessed Robert's condition and gave him oxygen. They then started him on a saline solution. I was in total shock. I just stood there as if I was in a movie. The medics gave Robert a heart massage and fresh oxygen. This could not be happening to us. Only minutes before, Robert and I were having the best sex of our marriage. Now I was watching my husband fight for his life. I have heard stories about men having heart attacks but I never thought that I would experience this first hand.

The medic got Robert's heart rate up and prepared to transport him to Decatur General. I told them I would follow as soon as I put on clothes. The medic took Robert out of the door and put him into the ambulance. I quickly put on my clothes and met them at the hospital. All the way there, I called my family members to let them know that Robert was being taken to the hospital. If Robert dies, I could not forgive myself. I would always have the image of him rolling off of me before I went to take a shower.

When I arrived in the emergency room, the doctor met me at entrance to the trauma center to explain what had happen to Robert. He had suffered a massive heart attack. They were taking scans to see if there was any blockage in his arteries. They had to put him on life support to help him breathe. I could not hold the tears back any longer. I collapsed right there in front of the doctor. He helped me to my feet escorting me to the waiting area. Shortly after, my arrival my mother and two sisters entered the waiting area. The doctor briefed them on Robert's condition as I lay in the chair crying.

"Don't worry baby. Everything will be all right," my mother said.

"I don't know mother. We were so happy and then this happened." I finally got the chance to spend some quality time with Robert and he has a heart attack."

"I know, child. The doctor says we can go in a see Robert. Do you have the strength?"

"Yes, mother."

The four of us went into the ICU to see Robert. He was lying there with his eyes closed and tubes in his mouth and arms. I could not believe what my eyes were seeing. Just an hour ago I was kissing Robert and feeling his love inside of me. Now, he was fighting for his life.

"Sit down my daughter, there is nothing you can do right now. It is in God's hands."

"Mother is right, Ann. We will stay with you tonight," said Lisa.

We all prayed in the small room hoping that this was a bad dream.

After we finished consoling each other, a nurse came in and informed us that only two visitors could remain in the room. The rest had to wait outside in the main waiting room. We all went together. I did not want to be alone. Lisa was curious as to what happened. I didn't want anyone to know the truth just yet.

"Robert was sitting on the sofa having a drink. When I returned from taking a shower, I found him on the floor. I called 911 and the rest is, as you know it. The doctor told me that he had a heart attack. It must be from the long hours he works. He never gets enough rest.

Tonight was the first night in a long time that he was home before me. We had planned a special evening. Then this happened.

"Girl, you have had your share of pain. It is not fair," said Mary.

"That is enough girls, we need to be positive and hope for the best," said my mother.

My mother and two sisters stayed with me all through the night. I routinely visited Robert holding his hand and saying a small prayer. God must have heard me. By morning, Robert was coming to. I saw his eyes open and he clinched my hands letting me know he was ok. I called the nurse to let them know that he was awake. The doctors came in to check his vital signs. Everything was looking up. Robert could not speak because the tubs were still in his mouth. The doctor said he would be able to take them out as soon as he finished his checks. He asked me to leave the room for a while and to come back in ten minutes. I ran to the waiting room and told my mother and two sisters the good news. Each of them grabbed my hands in joy.

"See, Ann, I told you everything would be alright."

"I know mother."

We all took turns going to see Robert. He was awake but incoherent. I told my family it was time to go. Robert would be able to get some rest and we all could get some sleep. Robert was out of danger and I wanted to come back to the hospital as fast as I could so I could be with him when he was more coherent. I kissed Robert on the forehead and said good night. I would return in a few hours to be by his side.

As I drove home, I could not help but blame myself for what happened to Robert. I knew in my heart that the long hours and his social drinking played a role, but I was the catalyst that started the process rolling. Robert was my life now and I didn't want anything to happen to him. I had almost forgotten to call Robert's parents. They would have never forgiven me if Robert had died.

I arrived at the home and quickly ran into the house. I changed clothes and headed back to the car. I couldn't stay at home while Robert was in the hospital. I would not be able to sleep. I still needed to call Roberts parents. I grabbed my cell phone from off the front passenger seat and dialed Robert's parent phone number.

"Hello."

"This is Ann, Barbara. I meant to call you hours ago but I was so hysterical. Robert is in the hospital but he is fine now. He just had a mild heart attack.

"He is ok you say."

"Yes Barbara, he is ok."

"Good, what happened?"

"I think he has been working to hard. We had dinner last night and a drink or two. When I came out of the bathroom he was on the floor. I called 911 and we went to the hospital."

"Well, I told you he was a hard worker that did not know how to take it easy. I knew the stress would catch up with him soon or later. I am so glad he is all right. I guess I should tell you that this is not his first heart attack."

"What!" I exhaled.

"Yes baby, Robert had a heart attack three years ago. He was doing ok until now. The doctor told him to exercise more and work less. I guess he is still putting in those long hours.

"Yes, he is. Sometimes I go to sleep and awake the next morning to find him in bed."

"You know I told you when you got married to Robert that he works a lot of hours. I should have told you that he had had a heart attack before because of his work schedule. I am sorry about not telling you Ann."

"It is ok, Barbara. It was Robert's task to tell me."

"I do wish I could come and see him. Please let me know how he is doing."

"I will."

"Call me when he can speak."

"I will."

"He knows I love him and I will pray that everything will be fine. I will let his father know. You know James can't drive far. If we could, we would come today."

"I understand fully, Barbara."

"James is afraid of flying." If he doesn't get better by tomorrow, we will have to fly down."

"No need to worry, Barbara. I just wanted to let you know. The doctor indicated that Robert would be ok. I will call you as soon as Robert can speak."

"Ok, baby. I will talk to you later."

As I ended my conversation with Barbara, I was arriving at the entrance to the ICU emergency room parking. It felt like I had been driving for days trying to make my way back to Robert. I quickly parked the car and ran into the hospital towards the ICU wing of the hospital. As I passed the nurses station, I noticed Robert was no longer in the room. I panicked as my heart rate went sky high. "Where is my husband?" I cried out. I fell to the floor in mental exhaustion.

"Miss, miss?" one of the nurses shouted while helping me to my feet.

"Where is my husband?"

"What is your husband's name, miss?

"His name is Robert Peterman."

"Miss, your husband is all right. We moved him to a private room about thirty minutes ago. We called, but did got get an answer at your home phone."

"I was on my way here."

"We were told that the doctor sent you home so we felt good about moving him. He is ok and recovering. The doctor is in the room with him now. Come with me and I will take you to him."

"Thank you. I thought that he was gone."

"No miss, he is strong and is recovering. Here is the room. Be calm because we don't want to get him excited. He has been though a major ordeal."

"Thank you so much," I said.

As I opened the door, Doctor Wilson met me.

"Mrs. Peterson, I hope you got some rest."

"Robert."

"He is fine. He is sleeping now. There are a few things I need to discuss with you."

"Ok. What is it Doctor Wilson?"

"Well, I did a little searching and found out that this is Robert's second heart attack. Were you aware that he had a heart problem?"

"No, Dr. Wilson, I was not aware until forty- five minutes ago when I spoke with his mother. Robert works hard and I guess he did not want me to get worried and talk to him about it."

"Well, Mrs. Peterman if Robert doesn't slow down and let his heart recover he will not be around to talk to you about his condition."

"What do you mean doctor?"

"Robert has scar tissue in his heart. It needs to heal or it may end up causing a blockage of his arteries. He must take off work for a few weeks so he can heal."

"No problem Doctor Wilson. I will take care of him and talk to his employer. He has a great boss."

"Ok, Mrs. Peterman. You can see him now. I will check back on him this afternoon before I leave for the day."

"Thanks, doctor."

"You are welcome, Mrs. Peterman."

I opened the door slightly to see Robert lying in bed with his eyes half opened. I eased over next to his bed setting in a chair positioned close to him.

"Ann, is that you?"

"Yes, Robert, I am here."

"That was a close one huh."

"What do you mean?"

"I almost bought the farm."

"Robert, don't play like that. We have to get you well. The doctor said you need to take it easy for a while."

"I know, Ann. I just need to take a week or two off so I can rest."

"You don't have to worry Robert. I will take care of you."

"I know you will baby."

"Oh, I told your mother I would call her when you could talk."

"Well, you can call her on that phone in the corner if you like."

"I will call her on my cell. I was able to call out last night and this morning."

"Ok, baby. What ever you say."

"Hello, Barbara. This is Ann."

"Hello, Ann. How is Robert?"

"You can ask him yourself Barbara."

"Hi,mom. I am doing fine."

"I am glad to hear that you are okay. I am not going to give you a lecture. I am so happy that you are ok. I told Ann I would get someone to take me to the airport if she needed my help with you."

"There is no need mother. I talked to the doctor and I will be just fine. I just need to take a week or two off."

"Ok, son. I believe Ann can take care of things. She is a good wife and a good person."

"I know mom. That is why I married her."

I kissed Robert on the lips as he continued talking to his mother.

"Well, mom I can't talk long. Tell Dad I am ok and I will call him when I get out of the hospital tomorrow."

"Good bye mom."

"Good bye, Robert."

Robert gave me the phone and closed his eyes. He was tired from the brief conversation he had with his mother. I sat beside Robert while he slept. So many thoughts went through my mind. I dreamed of work and everybody laughing and celebrating the opening of the new collections department. My mind went from one thought to another. I saw Douglas and Stephanie setting at the computer. I had almost forgot. I did not call Mr. Green to let him know I would not be coming to work. I had forgotten that I had a job. All of the activity with Robert sent my mind into overload. I quickly called Mr. Green.

"Hello, Mr. Green speaking."

"Hello, Mr. Green this is Ann Peterman."

"Hello, Ann. How are you?"

"I am fine Mr. Green. I am sorry for not coming to work today. My husband Robert was admitted to the hospital last night. I am currently at the hospital with him."

"Oh my dear! How is he?"

"He is out of trouble and resting right now."

"Ann, you take it easy and I will have Sheila sign you out on sick leave."

"Thank you so much, Mr. Green."

"No, allow me to thank you, Ann, for all you do. Take all the time you need. I know you will need the support of your family and the support of your co-workers."

"That is so true Mr. Green. Tell everyone the doctor said Robert will recover and be fine."

"Ok, I will."

As I hung up the phone, Robert opened his eyes again. I just sat and held his hands. He needed his rest. The doctor was planning to let him go in a few days as long as his vitals stayed normal. I knew Robert and I had a long road to travel towards his recovery.

~ CHAPTER TWENTY ~

Robert's Recovery

Robert was finally released from the hospital to come home. Today would be the first day of his long recovery. He looked fine from the outside; however, he had suffered mild paralysis on his left side. The doctor said he really needed to take it easy. As we arrived at the house, my family was there to greet us. I had asked Lisa to fly to Kentucky and bring back Robert's mother. They had arrived at the house just before Robert and I. Everyone was waiting in or near the door ready to help in any way they could.

"Mom?" Robert said softly. How did you get here?"

"Well it looks to me that you have a wonderful wife and a great extended family here in Georgia ready to take care of you. They extended themselves beyond their family's boundaries."

"You are right about that mom, they are great people. Where is dad?"

"He couldn't come. He wasn't feeling very well. He sends his love."

"Ok, everyone. Let me get Robert into the house," I said.

Everyone went into the house. Robert walked slowly over to the couch where he had been the night he had his heart attack. I looked into his eyes to see if he remembered anything. He sat and smiled politely at everyone. The doctor had mentioned to me that Robert had suffered from small memory lost. He may or may not remember what happened leading up to his heart attack.

"Thanks, Lisa, for bringing my mother here. I don't know if I will ever be able to repay you."

"No need to thank me Robert. My mother taught us to extend ourselves for family. I know you would have done the same."

"Yes, I would and I really appreciate your love and kindness. Thank you Lisa!"

"You are welcome Robert."

"So, Ann tells me that all of you were there the night I was admitted into the hospital."

"Yes we were," my family said in unison.

"There are not enough words to express my love for each of you. I only hope that I have an opportunity to display my gratitude."

My mother quickly seized the opportunity to speak and give a little wisdom.

"Robert, I know this heart attack was part of God's grand plan. God doesn't take you through a trial like this without a purpose. There is a message in it for you. I know you are a great provider and you love Ann very much. However, I think Ann would rather have you healthy and alive instead sick or dead. It is very important for you to look at what caused this heart attack and see if you can limit the stress that contributed to it."

"You are correct. I do need to limit my stress. I don't remember what I was doing that caused the heat attack. Ann, do you remember?"

"No, Robert. When I returned to the living room, you were on the floor."

"Where was I?"

"You were lying close to where you are now but near the head of the couch."

"Ok."

That was a close call. I didn't want to bring up the fact that Robert had a heart attack because we made love that evening. I know he would think about it each time we went to bed. He must never know. I am going to keep it a secret from him and my family. The last thing I need is everyone teasing me. I need to let this one fade into the sunset.

"Ann, I have cooked a very healthy meal," said Mom. "I hope you don't mind. I know everyone would be too tired to cook after the activities of the day."

"I am so glad mom. I am so happy that you came by. Why don't we all go into the dining room and eat."

"Yes, you are right Ann. I can eat a horse."

"Great, Robert. Please let mom help you to the table"

"Thanks, mom, but I can make it."

"Ok. Everyone sit down and eat."

My mother said a long prayer. It was a day that we all would remember.

~ Chapter Twenty-One ~

A Friend's Help

"Did you hear about Ann's husband?"

"No, Tony. Did I hear what about Ann's husband?"

"He had a heart attack, Mr. Brown."

"Robert had a heart attack?"

"Yes! Haven't you noticed that Ann was not here yesterday and today?"

"Yes, I have noticed. I figured she was out on leave with Robert on a trip or something. He is always going somewhere."

"Not this time, Mr. Brown. Her husband almost went somewhere permanently."

"How do you know all this Tony?"

"I heard Mr. Green talking to Flora this morning. They will be taking up a collection to send them a fruit basket."

"Well, you let me know whatever they decide to do."

"I will, Mr. Brown."

That boy always knows what is happening around here before anyone else. You have to put in a sound system to stay ahead of him. I wonder why no one has sent an email out informing us about Ann. It would have been the most appropriate thing to do. No matter, I will call Ann myself and see if she needs my support in any way.

"Douglas! Can I talk to you for a moment?"

"Yes, Mr. Green."

"Have a seat. I just wanted to let you know that Ann will be working from home for a week or two and would like for you to arrange courier transportation to take her assigned projects to and from her house."

"Why me instead of Flora?"

"Well, Flora will have her hands full with the new collection department. I know that Ann and you are good friends and she may need your assistance from time to time until her husband recovers. He will probably not be able to do much for a month or two. Ann is such a valued employee and this is just our way of saying we are here for you."

"Okay, Mr. Green. I will call Ann and ask if she needs anything."

"Thanks so much Douglas. I can always depend on you."

"No problem, Mr. Green."

Well, isn't this a turn of events. I thought no one knew what the hell was happening with Ann and to find out that I have been pegged to be the proxy husband. I better call Ann to see what if anything I can do.

"Hello?"

"Yes, may I speak to Ann?"

"Who shall I say is calling?"

"Tell her it is Douglas Brown from the office."

"Okay, Mr. Brown. She is with Robert right now. I am Robert's mother. I will tell her you called."

"Thanks a million and we hope Robert will make a full recovery."

"Okay, I will tell Ann you called."

Well, that went great, here I am hoping to speak to Ann and see if there is anything I can do and her mother-in-law answered the phone. I hope she doesn't think I was trying to make a move. Mother-in-laws can be quite defensive when it comes to their daughter-in-laws. No matter. I will talk to Ann when she calls. Besides, I have a million things to do since we opened the new center. There was a knock at the door.

"Who is it now?"

"Douglas, may I come in?"

"Yes, Flora. Please have a seat."

"I spoke with Mr. Green and she informed me that you would be taking Ann her assignments."

"Yes, you are correct."

"Well, I have put together a packet for her. I have included instructions for everything in the packet. I also want you to give her this laptop to use. It is already set up for wireless email. She will just have to plug in this module. I hope you don't mind if I go over everything with you just in case she has any questions."

"No, Flora. I am more than happy to assist you and Ann during this period of recovery of her husband. Ann and I are good friends."

"Douglas, I really appreciate all your help."

"No problem. I get paid to provide support for each program in the department."

"No, what I mean you have helped me raise the bar when it comes to men. I use to think that I could use my looks to get what I want. I had low self-esteem. I guess all the time I tried to get you in bed made me realize that maybe I needed to re-evaluate my priorities. If I wasn't good enough for you then I needed to put myself in a position so that a man like yourself would see the same thing in me that you saw in Stephanie and what you see in Ann. Sometimes it takes a real man telling you up front that he is not interested in you in order for a girl to really take a good look at herself and see what is wrong."

"Well, Flora, I didn't mean to hurt your feelings or anything. I just I didn't feel any chemistry between us. I don't see anything wrong with you. You are attractive. I go on my intuition when I meet someone I am interested in."

"I see your point. I guess most people do."

"Anyway, I am glad you feel the way you do now. I had a similar experience with a girl. The situation caused me to close down and not date anyone for a long time. I had to take a really good look at myself. I thought I was a worthy catch; however, the other person thought differently. So, today and for the rest of my life, I will live one day at a time hoping to find Ms. Right. I am not ready to jump into anything serious."

"I know what you mean, Douglas. Tell Ann if she has any questions to give me a call."

"Okay, Flora, I will." Flora left my office and I sat down for a little self-reflection. Well, isn't that great. Flora has turned over a new leaf. Maybe Mr. Tuesday has really made a commitment to her. Whatever the case, I am glad for her.

It wasn't thirty-seconds after Flora left my office that the phone rang. It was Ann.

"Hello, Douglas. How are you?"

"Great, Ann. I am doing find. How is Robert? I hope all is well."

"Robert is recovering. He seems to be fine. We will know more as he starts to recover his memory. The doctor said it would take a few weeks before he starts to regain his short term memory functions."

"I am so glad to hear that he is doing fine."

"So, how is having your mother-in-law there helping?"

"It is great. She is taking some of the pressure off me when I have to run to the store or take care of the bills. She is truly a blessing. However, she will be leaving tomorrow because she has to return to take care of her husband."

"I understand."

"So, why did you call, Douglas?"

"Oh, I am sorry. Mr. Green asked me to be the official courier for your projects. I will drop them off and pick them up. Also, he wanted me to help out if you needed things moved or lifted. Robert made a big impact with the donations from his company in support of the opening of the new collections department. It is just Mr. Green's way of saying thank you."

"Ok, I see. I really appreciate you volunteering. I could use a little help. I will call you after my mother-in-law leaves to set up a time you can come by and lend both Robert and myself a hand."

"That sounds great, Ann. I would be more than happy to help out in any way I can." I almost forgot Ann. Flora asked me to drop a package by your house tomorrow."

"Yes, that will be fine."

"Okay, do you know where I live?

"I have your address. I think I will be able to find your house. Tell Robert that we all are praying for him and wishing he has a speedy recovery."

"Okay, Douglas, thanks again for being a friend."

"Ann, it is my pleasure."

After I finished talking to Ann, I thought about how I would avail myself to assist her. I needed to take care of all my duties in the morning and drop by her house sometime in the afternoon.

~ Chapter Twenty-Two ~

Douglas at Ann's House

"Thanks for coming by, Douglas."

"No problem Ann. I am happy to help out. How is Robert?"

"He is fine. I just took him for his check up today. He will be at the doctor's office undergoing tests all afternoon. I told him I had to return home and work on a project to go back to the office today. He was ok with me leaving."

"Well that is great, Ann. I was hoping to say hello. I haven't seen him since the grand opening of the new department. Please tell him I said hello."

"I will, Douglas. We can sit at the kitchen table. I have almost finished with the reports. However, I did have a few questions concerning the network security for the collections department's data."

"Yes, I understand. I have discussed the feasibility of securing the data with a new software program that has its own firewall. Mr. Green has forwarded an addendum to the budget department requesting additional funding."

"Well, that answered all my questions on network security. Tell Flora I have enclosed a comprehensive list of reoccurring delinquent accounts. If she has any questions she can call me and I will go over the list with her."

"Okay, I will take everything and review it with her. Is there anything else you need me to do? The last time I was here you needed me to cut the lawn. I brought along a change of clothes just in case."

"Well, I could use a little help."

"Fine that settles it. By the way, how is your mother-in-law? When I dropped her off at the airport she seemed like she was developing a cold."

"She is ok. I really appreciate you helping me with her. All my family was busy that day and I really didn't want to leave Robert alone. It has been a month now and he still hasn't fully recovered. He was very weak when he got out of bed today. I didn't want to leave him at the therapist's office but I had to get some things accomplished before Mrs. Green calls me back to work."

"No problem, Ann. I am more than happy to help you in any way I can."

"I know, Douglas, thanks so much."

Ann leaned towards me and gave me a big bear hug. I accepted it like a child being hugged by his mother. I pressed my chest firmly against her. I felt her heart beating rapidly as she released the hug, giving me a big smile while looking into my eyes for a reaction. I returned her smile thinking to myself how excited I was. I was alone with the women I wanted to make love to. I had dreamed about this exact moment for years. I stood there thinking how wonderful it would be if Ann was my wife.

"Douglas, are you ok?"

"Yes, Ann. I'm all right why did you ask."

"Well, you seemed to be in a daze. I asked you if you were ready to change clothes and you didn't respond."

"Oh…I'm sorry I was just thinking about something. I will go and get my clothes out of the car."

"Douglas, you can change in the bathroom located down the hall. I am going to put on a pair of work jeans. Let yourself out and back in. I will make it quick."

"Okay, Ann."

I quickly unlocked the front door and went to my car to get my clothes. As I returned, I passed the master bedroom where Ann was. She had just started to take off her clothes. I know I should have continued to walk pass her door. She had just entered into the master bath. Her back was facing her bedroom. There was a large mirror on the wall that caught her reflection allowing me to see. I stood there as she pulled her blouse over her head. She faced toward her bedroom and I saw her lean forward to let her skirt fall to the floor. She stood there in all her glory. I soldiered up with my two-by-four. I couldn't take it any more. I hurried to the bathroom and put on my work clothes. As I finished dressing, sweat had begun to build up on my forehead. I heard Ann coming down the hall.

"Douglas, is everything ok?"

"Yes, Ann. I'll be out in a second."

I finished putting on my shoes and came out of the bathroom. Ann had on a long t-shirt that hugged her outline. She was very sexy. I looked at her wishing she were mine. I really had to contain myself.

"Douglas, I need you to help me put some boxes of old clothes up in the attic."

I was ready to do anything she asked. I knew in my heart I shouldn't have these feelings, but they just poured out without any help from me.

"So where is your attic, Ann?" I asked the question simply to take my mind off her body.

"It is in the hallway next to the master bedroom."

I could feel my heartbeat quicken as I moved back to the spot that I saw Ann take her clothes off. I felt my excitement coming back. I had to do something quick. But I didn't know what to do.

"Douglas, can you get those boxes out of my bedroom. They are around the corner near the left side of the bed."

I started to sweat again. I quickly retrieved the boxes and exited her bedroom.

"Are you okay, Douglas?" Ann said jokingly.

"I will be okay as soon as we finish storing these boxes."

"All right," Ann said as she pulled the string to let the attic stairs fall down.

"I will go first," Ann said.

I stood at the base of the ladder hiding my excitement underneath the boxes. I observed Ann moving from left to right as she ascended the stairs. I wanted to take a big juicy bite out of her. Instead, I handed her the boxes as we both entered into the hot attic. Now the both of us started to sweat as we moved boxes from one side to the other. I could see a small ring of water starting to make an outline of Ann's chest. It was simply torture being in the hot attic with Ann.

"Are you okay, Douglas?"

"Yes, I'm okay Ann. Why do you keep asking me if I am okay?"

"I am truly sorry, Douglas. Let's finish with the boxes and I will tell you why."

By this time, I couldn't wait to get out of the attic. We had been in there for fifteen minutes moving boxes and old furniture from one side of the room to the other. We were both soaked with sweat when we came down the ladder.

"I really appreciate you helping me, Douglas."

"It was no problem at all, Ann."

"Let me get you something to drink."

"Water would be nice."

"As I was saying, the reason I kept asking you if you were ok is because Robert had his heart attack in the den. It stays on my mind. I have never told anyone what really happened. I don't think Robert even remember what happened. The doctor said he would not remember anything leading up to his heart attack. We have not made love since that night."

"You mean that Robert had a heart attack while he was making love to you?"

"No not exactly, he had a heart attack afterward, while I was in the shower."

"So why are you putting all the blame on yourself, Ann?"

"I don't know Douglas. I guess I found him there and it seemed as if it was my fault."

"I don't think it was your fault. It takes two to tango and if Robert was under stress it probably was going to happen with you or without you. You see, a lot of times your mate tends to take on a lot of the pressures caused by their partners. It is important to talk to someone and get another opinion so you can look at the situation clearly."

"You are so right, Douglas."

Ann leaned forward to give me a hug. It was just what I needed. I didn't hold anything back. I pulled her close and as I was releasing her I looked into her eyes and expressed my feeling right then and there. I didn't say anything but I let her see what was inside of me. Ann gave me a small kiss on the mouth and released me. She held my hand like I was her big brother.

"Oh…my, look at the time. I need to get across town to pick up Robert."

"Okay, Ann, I will give you a call later on in the week. If you need me to bring you anything, please call and let me know."

"That's great. I have to take Robert back to the therapist on Thursday. Do you think you can come by and help me in the yard?"

"I'll be here."

I grabbed my clothes and headed for the front door. Just before I left, Ann approached me at the door and gave me the kiss I had only hoped I had received when I first met her. When she let go I was surprised and ecstatic. Ann just smiled at me as I went out the door. I didn't know what to say. I sat in her driveway for a few minutes, wondering if I should go back and knock on the door.

I soon recovered from the effects of the kiss and headed back to the office. I even forgot to ask Ann to take a shower. It was a good thing that I only had a thirty-minute drive and thirty me left at work. I thought long and hard about that kiss and made sure I eliminated every possible answer that it could be nothing more than a friendly kiss. That particular kiss could get you in trouble if you don't understand its intent.

Well, I soon arrived back to the office and flopped down in my awaiting chair. My mind was spinning out of control; however, that to soon ended. Just when I was about to have the daydream of my life, Flora knocked on the door.

"Good afternoon, Douglas."

"Hello, Flora. What's up? How are you today?"

"I am great, Douglas."

"Here are the reports Ann sent. She said if you had any questions to give her a call."

"Thank you so much, Douglas. You have really helped us a lot this past month. I hope Ann has appreciated what you have done for her."

"I am quite sure she knows. Besides, I am only doing my job. I would do the same thing for any of the employees."

"I guess you would, Douglas. I really have to admire you. You treat everyone the same"

"I figure it is easier to be happy if you treat everyone like you want to be treated. You know the phrase 'Do unto others as you would have them do unto you.' "

"Douglas, now that is a great truth."

"You are so right. However, it is hard to treat other people like you would like to be treated if they are bad natured."

"I know. I just don't let folks get to me."

"Yeah, you are right."

"Well, thanks again, Douglas. I'll let you know what additional reports we need to send Ann."

"Okay, Flora."

Finally, I sat back and reflected on what happened at Ann's house. If I can't have her, I can at least savor and enjoy this one moment in time. Although, I cannot believe I let Ann get away with that kiss. She is lucky that Robert was waiting on her. I would have spanked that booty like it needed to be spanked.

Suddenly, I stopped thinking about Ann and started to think about what I had told Flora. I guess I really needed to understand the phrase "Treat others like you want them to treat you." I had forgotten all about Robert.

~ Chapter Twenty-Three ~

Robert's Treatment

"Well Mr. Peterman, it seems that you are making good progress."

"Thanks doctor. I have been really taking it easy. Ann has been taking very good care of me. She is concerned that I will return to work and stress myself out again."

"Robert, it is important that you make a life-style change so you won't have another heart attack."

"You're so right about that Mrs. Peterman. It is important that you keep your stress level to a minimum, Robert. We do not want you to get too excited and have a return visit to the hospital. You may not be as lucky next time."

"I understand doctor. I will take it easy. I wish I knew what caused this heart attack. I cannot for the life of me remember what lead up to the attack."

"I fear you may never remember, Robert."

"What do you remember, Ann? "

"That is the first time you have asked me Robert. I remember coming into the room after taking a shower to find you on the floor. I had been at the opening ceremonies for the dedication of the new collection department at work. When I returned home to relax and have a drink, I found you lying on the floor when I came out of the shower."

"Well doctor, there you have it. I wasn't even at my own job when this happened. It was not a result of my work that caused me to go belly up."

"I see, Robert. I still need you to go to your therapy section this afternoon. I hope to release you to go back to work pretty soon."

"Okay, Dr. Wilson. I will be more than happy to go to therapy if I can go back to work. I am ready to get back in the game."

"Ok, sweetheart. We need to get you well first and then you can play as much ball as you like."

"Okay, Robert. I will see you next month. I hope the test results will be favorable."

"Thank you so much doctor. I'll make sure Robert takes it easy until then."

"Good-bye Doc," Robert said.

Robert and I left the doctor's office. He was feeling a little better about returning to work. I needed to drop him off at the therapist and meet Douglas at my house.

"Ok, Robert. I'll pick you up at 3:30 p.m. I need to finish a report to send back to work. You can call me when you finish. Remember, Douglas will drop by and cut the lawn today. He said to tell you hello."

"I hope I will be finished in time. If I am not let him know how much I appreciate his help. He has been a true friend. I wish I had a co-worker like him."

"Ok, sweetheart."

Now that I have finished with my morning chores, I can get back to the house and complete the report before Douglas arrives. I hope he will be able to help me get a couple of things done today. I really enjoyed the time I spent with him last week. He didn't know that I saw him looking at me in my bedroom. I got really turned on knowing he was there. He didn't even mention the kiss I gave him. He probably thought it was just a friendly peck. I have been without some good loving for a month. I am afraid that if I get with Robert, he will have another heart attack. I don't want to have an affair. I just need a little attention. Douglas could give me what I needed if I asked.

What am I talking about! I am a married woman. Robert has given me the world. Besides, in a few weeks Robert will be able to take care of me. But it would be great if Douglas would take those big manly hands of his and give me a massage. I would kiss him so deeply that he would know exactly what a girl needed. Boy, that would be great. What am I saying? These are thoughts I really need to keep to myself.

Well, look who is already here. Douglas has already cut the front lawn. I wonder if he is thirsty. I don't believe it. I only need to daydream and it comes to life. I better finish my report while he working. I slowly parked my car into the garage without him knowing. I ran into the shower to freshen up.

When I came out of the shower I heard the doorbell ring. I guess Douglas did see me as I drove into the garage. I quickly put on my bathrobe and went to the door.

"Hello, Ann," he said.

"I hope you do not mind that I started to cut the grass before you got back. I must return to the office early today. I knocked on the door when I arrived but I didn't get an answer. I assumed that you and Robert had gone to his appointment. The garage door was unlocked, so I got the lawn mower out and start cutting the grass.

"Oh. There is no problem Douglas. Would you like a towel or a glass of water?"

"A glass of water would be fine. I was hoping Robert would be here so I could take a shower."

"Why is that?"

"You know...protocol."

"I think it will be alright for you to take a shower Douglas. I will get you a face and body towel. It is ok. Besides it will give me an opportunity to finish my report. I only have to add a few cost figures."

"Are you sure it will not be a problem?"

"It is not a problem Douglas. Letting you take a shower is the least I can do considering all you have done for me this past month."

"Well, okay. Is there anything else you need me to do before I get cleaned up?"

"No I am fine right now."

As Douglas was walking away, I opened my housecoat slightly so he could get a good peek. I watched him as his eyes made contact and open widely. I turned away making sure he saw me as I walked towards the kitchen table. Douglas hurried into the bathroom. I took my time finishing the report. I was hoping that Douglas came out of the shower with nothing but the towel wrapped around him. I took the time to sit facing the hallway that Douglas would walk down. I let my bathrobe hang off the high part of my thigh. I waited patiently for Douglas to come.

"Ann, can you hand me my shirt I left on the sofa?" he called out.

"Okay, Douglas."

I retrieved Douglas's shirt and headed down the hallway. My heart started to beat faster with each step I took. I imagined Douglas waiting there with his chest full of hair and naked as a jaybird. As I arrived at the door, Douglas only stuck his hand out waving it for me to put the shirt in it.

"Thanks, Ann."

I gave Douglas his shirt and turned away in disappointment. I walked back down the hallway and put the finishing touches on the report.

All during my drive home, I had hoped to entice Douglas into making a pass at me. The only thing I got was a hand waving out of the bathroom door. Maybe Flora was right. Douglas is a scary cat. Here he has the chance of a lifetime to seduce me and he will not make one pass at me. I don't believe it.

"Thanks, Ann, for the shower."

"It was nothing. I would have allowed any field hand to take a shower."

"Excuse me! What did you say?"

"I didn't say anything Douglas."

"Yes you did, Ann."

"I am sorry, Douglas. I lost control for a moment. I was expecting you to make a pass at me and when you didn't I got angry."

"Ann, you know better than that. I would take you right now if I could have you for my own. However, you and Robert have some issues to work out. You have to get over your fear of Robert having another heart attack. Once you do, your love life will return to normal."

"I know, Douglas. There is a part of me that is so afraid of making love to him. Every time Robert holds me close I see that night over and over in my mind. It is hard for me to feel like I use to."

"I know, Ann. If I could help you I would. You must travel this road with Robert. If things don't work out, I will be there waiting for you. I don't want to have you like this. I want to earn the right to be your husband if the opportunity presents itself."

"How can any woman resist your charm Douglas? You are a good friend. Here I was ready to give you all of this and you stand strong beside me making me do the right thing."

"I am not strong, Ann. I just love you enough to say no. Ann, there is one more thing."

"What is it Douglas?"

"You have a very nice tattoo."

"I know you saw me and you didn't say anything."

"I wasn't aware that you knew I saw you. Besides, you were not supposed to know I saw you."

Douglas and I had a good laugh. I gave him the report to take back to the office. He wouldn't accept any loving from me, but I managed to give him a repeat of the kiss I had given him during the week. I understood what he meant. Love is forever. He has me in his heart. That is where he wants to keep me for now.

~ Chapter Twenty-Four ~

Something Unexpected

On the way back to the office, I found myself in a good mood. I had finally confronted my feelings for Ann and let her know how I really felt. I had the perfect opportunity to make love to her but decided to love her as a friend instead. Sometimes you got to go with your gut feelings instead of the feelings below your guts. I know I will always wonder how great the encounter would have been, but for now I can move on knowing that I had the opportunity of a life time and did the right thing.

As I entered the entrance to the office, I saw Sheila standing at the receptionist's desk with a big smile on her face.

"So…I see that you have returned, Douglas."

"Hello, Sheila. How are you today?"

"Someone has received several calls from a long lost friend."

"Okay, Sheila, what do you mean by that."

"I forwarded the calls to your phone."

"Well, Ms. Sheila is that all you had to say. I guess I will know as much as you when I take the messages off the answering machine."

"I guess you will."

Who could have possibly called me that Sheila knows? Maybe it was Ann calling to say thank you or something. I guess I will see soon enough. Well, there are not any notes on the door. I better check my answering machine.

"Hello, Douglas, this is Stephanie. I know this call will come as a surprise to you but I have a very good reason for calling. It has been two years since I last saw you and it is time we say hello again. I will be in Atlanta on Tuesday of next week. I will call you before I arrive. There is something I need to tell you."

That was the end of the message. What can she possibly mean? What does she have to tell me? On one of the greatest days of my life I get two surprises. I guess when it rains it pours. But why would Stephanie come back to Atlanta to see me? Could it be she remembered how great Miami was and wants to rekindle an old fire? Now that would be great.

I need to get these thoughts out of my mind. How can I possibly think of Stephanie when I have just denied myself the greatest wish I could have received? I had the opportunity of a lifetime. I could have had Ann in my arms kissing her, holding her, and making sweet love to her. I cannot believe I let this once in a lifetime opportunity get away from me. All these years I have hoped, waited, and sometimes prayed that Ann would give me the time of day. As soon as she told me what time it was, I panicked and did the moral thing. I really need to get my head screwed on right. Sometimes it is ok to be selfish. If she ever asks me to make love to her again, I will not hesitate. As a matter of fact, I am going to call her and let her know I am available to come over there and help out next week if she needs me.

Where is her number?

"Hello, you have reached the Peterman's. Please leave a message after the beep."

"Ann this is Douglas. I have a few questions concerning your report can you give me a call at the office. I will be here until five o'clock today. Thank you. Well that went great. Here I stand with all the nerves in the world and no one to show I have them. That just goes to prove I should always go on my first instinct. Telephone ringing in the background!

"Hello, Douglas Brown speaking."

"Well hello, Douglas. You are a hard person to catch up to."

"And this is?"

"You don't remember my voice Douglas?"

"Ann!"

"No, Douglas this is not the number three person. I am the number two person. Remember, I am next in line behind Mr. Green.

"Oh Stephanie!"

"How are you doing?"

"I am okay, Douglas. Did you get my messages?"

"Yes, I just listened to them an hour ago."

"So why are you coming back to 'Hot Atlanta?'

"Well, like I said, I have a surprise for you."

"A surprise, huh?"

"Yes, a surprise. I was able to take care of my kids and get them settled with their father and now I am able to take care of an issue I have with you."

"So where have you been staying all this time?"

"As you know when I left, my mother moved back to California with me. We decided to save money by living together. So, I have been living with her for the last two years. My kids live with their father now. It was for the best, right now. He has remarried a nice woman and they have a child of their on. It makes perfect sense to let them spend some time growing up with them."

"Well, that sounds great Stephanie. When did you say you would be flying in?"

"I will arrive in Atlanta at two o'clock on Tuesday. Can you pick me up?"

"Yes, no problem."

"I also do not have a place to stay. Do you mind letting me stay with you for a few days. I will be leaving on Friday returning to California."

"You know you can stay with me as long as you like."

"Douglas, you are the best. I will call you on Monday to confirm."

"Stephanie, there is no problem. I will make myself available to you during the time you are here. I need a little vacation. What else do you plan on doing?"

"Nothing much, I am coming just to see you."

"Fine I will be yours during the time you are here."

"Douglas, I am really looking forward to seeing you."

"I feel the same Stephanie. I can't wait to see what the surprise is."

"You don't have to worry. I haven't bothered you in two years, have I."

"No, you have not. I will look forward to your call on Monday. Take care."

"Okay, Douglas. I will call you on Monday. Good Bye!"

Well, I cannot imagine what this surprise can be. No matter, I will see soon enough. Anyway, it will be nice to see Stephanie again. It has been too long. I am ready for this friendly reunion. Dam! I better call Ann back and tell her I will be busy next week so she can arrange for me to take care of what ever she needs me to do tomorrow or this weekend. Where is her number? I need to get a phone date book or something.

"Hello."

"Hello, Robert! How are you?"

"Fine and this is?"

"Douglas! I am the operation manager from Ann's office."

"Yes, Douglas! Ann has told me that you have helped her a lot around the house and with her work projects. She also told me that you asked about me each time you came by. I really appreciate all you and your office have done for us."

"You are welcome. It was our pleasure to help out in any way we could. Ann is a valuable employee. Mr. Green and the staff really appreciate her work."

"That is great. I never had the opportunity to say thanks for the cards and fruit basket that your office sent."

"We were glad to wish you a speedy recovery."

"Well, I am well on my way to going back to work. The therapist gave me a clean bill of health today. I will call my doctor tomorrow and see if he releases me. I have to get back on the job. You know what I mean, don't you, Douglas."

"I guess I do, Robert."

"By the way, the grass looks nice. You cut it just the way I cut it. I really appreciate your helping out. I don't think it wise for me to get out in the sun and stress myself right away. I hope I will be able to repay you one day."

"Don't mention it, Robert. I was happy to help out. Ann is a very nice lady and she has a wonderful guy taking care of her. The both of you are good people. I was fortunate to have had the opportunity to lend a helping hand. By the way, is Ann there?"

"I am sorry, Douglas. I got so excited about thanking you I forgot that you wanted to speak to Ann."

"She is not here. She got your message off the answering machine and muttered something about calling you later."

"Okay, that is great. Tell her I called and that if she or you need help this weekend to let me know. I have to be off next week to help out a friend."

"Okay, Douglas. Thanks again for all your help."

"Good bye, Robert.

Dam! I guess that is the end of that. However, there is a pot of gold at the end of this rainbow. Her name is Stephanie. I may have to wait a few days, but I will be able to collect my gold.

~ Chapter Twenty-Five ~

Ann Returns To Work

So, what do you think Ann? Can I still put the icing on the cake?" –Said in a low voice

"Yes, but it was smeared all over the place."

"What did you say?"

"Yes, Robert. However, I was scared the entire time. I was afraid that you would have another heart attack.

"What do you mean another heart attack?"

"I didn't want to say anything before because I didn't want to worry you or relive that night. You had your heart attack after the last time we made love. It was the same night that my job opened the new collections department."

"That is why you were squirming while we made love?

"Yes."

"Come here baby. If I had a heart attack while we made love, you shouldn't worry or feel bad. It would be the ideal way to go. Love me for the here and now. Tomorrow is not promised to you or me. We promised to love each other for as long as we both shall live."

"I know, Robert, but I couldn't get the thoughts out of my mind that I caused it."

"No baby. You didn't cause it. I have a mild heart condition. I had it before I met you. As a result of my work environment, I have developed a higher risk factor. My work environment is quite stressful; however, the rewards are great. But for you my Ann, I promise to take it easy."

"Okay, Robert. Remember you promised to take it easy."

"I just said I promise. Come here and give me a kiss before you go to work."

"Okay!"

Shortly afterward, I left the house headed back to work. The quickie Robert got did not completely satisfy my deep burning desire for relief. All during the drive to work, I thought of Douglas. I could almost feel his hands gently giving me a massage. Every time I thought of him, I started to sweat. I should have taken it from him the day he was at my house. I wanted him so bad. I will never get another opportunity. The thoughts will always hunt me. Well, I guess it is no use thinking about what will never be.

As I drove up in the parking lot, Sheila and the gang were headed to the office's front entrance.

"Hello Ann," all of them said together.

"Hi," I said to Sheila, Cynthia, Flora, and Tonya."

Each greeted me with a big hug and happy faces acknowledging their delight to see me. I quickly greeted everyone accordingly and went to my office. I really did appreciate each of them and the love they have shown; however, I was more concerned about seeing Douglas. I needed to see him and talk to him. Only he could relieve me of the frustration I carried. I couldn't get rid of my desire for Douglas. I tried to get the thoughts out of my mind. I know, Robert is ok now and can take care of my needs. Although, when a woman gets an itch for a certain man her desire to have him increases with every thought. There is only one man that can extinguish this fire.

I finally made it to my office. I couldn't believe that I was consumed with these feelings for Douglas. As I sat in my chair, I imagined him kissing me. I thought of losing total control as he held me in his arms. I must have blanked out for a moment because I couldn't remember what happened next. Suddenly there was a knock on the door.

"Ann, are you in there?" I heard Mr. Green call out.

"Yes, I am Mr. Green."

I quickly got up from the chair and opened the door.

"Welcome back, Ann!"

"Thanks, Mr. Green. I really appreciate all the support you and the entire staff gave to Robert and me."

"I was very happy to be of assistance. Everyone enjoys having you here. You are a great person as well as a great employee. When one of our families members is in need we must all reach out to help."

"I really appreciated your support. Douglas was of great help too. However, I haven't seen him in the office this morning."

"You are right Ann. Douglas took three days off. He won't be back to work until Monday."

"Monday!" I said aloud.

"Did you say something Ann?"

"No, Mr. Green I was clearing my throat."

"Oh, well. I am glad you are back and that Robert has recovered."

"Thank you so much, Mr. Green. I am ready to get back to work and I am looking forward to the challenges of the of my department."

"Okay, Ann. I will see you later."

"Good bye, Mr. Green."

I really appreciated what Mr. Green did for Robert and me; however, he caught me at a very bad moment. I had just finished getting my Douglas on when he knocked on the door. I still need to go to the bathroom and clean my hands. Now I discover that Douglas will not be here for the next three days. This is twice that he has done this to me. I just can't turn this feeling off unless he gives me what I need.

"Ann, its Sheila. May I come in?"

"Yes, Sheila. I am sorry for rushing into the office this morning. I needed a little time by myself. It has been two months since I have been at work. I need to relax and figure out how to get back into the rhythm of things."

"I understand completely, Ann. I just wanted to say hello and give you the 411 on Douglas."

"What do you mean the 411 on Douglas?"

"Well, while you were out a certain Ms. Somebody called to speak to Douglas."

"Who?"

"I believe it was Stephanie."

"After all this time!"

"Yes, I took the call and put it though to his office myself."

"So that explains why he is taking leave this week."

"I guess so Ann. He did seem a little happy the last time I saw him."

"Thanks, Sheila, is that all?"

"No, Ann. We are going to have a coming back luncheon in your honor today and we were hoping you could come."

"Yes, I can make it. I need to get busy and return a few emails. Tell everyone thanks a lot and I will see each of them at lunch."

"Are we eating at our usual spot?"

"Yes, at our usual spot. I will drive today Ann."

"Okay, Sheila, I will see you when we get ready to leave."

Well, now, isn't that a big surprise. Here I am masturbating over Douglas and he is renewing an old fling with Stephanie. I guess I need to get these thoughts out of my mind and concentrate on my job and on Robert. Douglas and I will never happen. It is all a pipe dream. I need to get control of myself and move on. Besides, I will be going to lunch soon and need to have my head screwed on properly.

~ CHAPTER TWENTY-SIX ~

Lunch with the Girls

It is time to go Ann," said Sheila as she peeked inside my door.

"Is it 12:00 already?"

"Yes it is and I am starving."

"So Ann, how has your morning been going?"

"Great so far, I only received one phone call and that was from Robert wishing me a good day at work."

"So how is Robert?"

"Robert is doing fine. He will be returning to work next week. The doctor will release him off medical leave starting next Monday."

"That is great, Ann. He gave us all a scare. We prayed hard for the both of you. We all were so happy when he was released from the hospital."

"Yes, I was too. I really appreciate all the support Robert and I received from the staff. It was just great. I don't think I can ever repay everyone."

"Hey, don't mention it. Just hope we don't hit you up for lunch today."

"Don't mention it, Ann. That is the least that I can do. By the way, is everyone joining us for lunch?"

"I think so."

Sheila and I left the building. All of the ladies saw us and ran over to the car. Tonya, Cynthia, and Flora jumped into the back seat. All of them were asking so many questions that I couldn't answer one question before someone asked another. I finally told them that we could discuss everything over lunch. They calmed down and permitted the entire group to discuss work topics for a moment.

"So, Ann, I heard you were looking for Douglas this morning," asked Flora.

"Yes, I was Flora. I wanted to thank him for the help he gave me during the last two months."

"Well you know Douglas. I had a good long conversation with him about guys and why I have had a new look on life because of him."

"What do you mean, Flora?"

"Well, let us just say that Douglas is the reason I had a steady man in my life."

"Is Douglas your man?" asked Sheila.

"No, Douglas is not my man but his rejection taught me a good lesson about self- esteem. I had fallen as low as I could possible go. I was able to realize that by throwing myself at a man is not the correct way to get a man to like me. After all the times Douglas turned me down he never insulted me or made me lose my self-esteem. I can now play the dating game like it supposed to be played. I have a new lease on life and a new awareness about the woman I'm supposed to be."

"Well, that is great Flora. I would like to hear more when we get inside."

We all exited the car and you could not guess who we saw leaving the parking lot like he did not see us. It was Douglas. There was a lady with long black hair sitting on the passenger side.

"Can you believe that? He acted like we were not standing here," said Tonya.

I thought he probably had other things on his mind. Well, we dismissed the situation and went into the restaurant and as faith would have it, we sat in our favorite booth. We even got the same waitress that normally serves us.

"Well Ann! I haven't seen you around here in a while. I hope all is well."

"Yes, Chiquita, all is well. Thank you so much for asking."

"You are so welcome. Now, what can I get for you ladies today?" I know the usual. Flora and Cynthia will have the fried chicken salad, one with ranch and one with honey mustard. Sheila will have the chicken tenders with fries. Tonya and Ann will have the fried chicken salad with salmon instead of the chicken."

"I see you haven't forgotten a thing, Chiquita." I said as she picked up the menus.

"No I haven't. You ladies are a pleasure to serve. The five of you have real class."

"Why, thank you very much, I said preparing to answer the multitude of questions that the group was ready to throw at me.

"Okay, wait just a minute before everyone asks a million questions;" I said trying to preempt the group. "I will start from the beginning and you can ask questions based on what I tell you."

"Okay," everyone said.

"Let me see where I will start. Robert's heart attack happened after he and I left the grand opening for the collections department two months ago. We were at home having a quiet dinner. I had picked up a couple of fresh salads from Chick-fil-A. We were listening to some Luther Vandross and enjoying the evening. I later went to take a shower and when I returned, he was on the floor trying to catch his breath. I called the ambulance and they took him to the hospital. I followed in my car totally out of it. We arrived at the hospital at the same time.

"Girl, I know you didn't," said Sheila.

"Yes, my adrenaline level was high. I went into the emergency room where they would not let me see him until they took him to ICU. I called my family and they stayed with me until the doctor encouraged me to get some sleep. The doctor said he would call me immediately if anything changed. So, I went home at about 4:00 a.m. and arrived back at the hospital at 9.a.m. that morning. I cried all the way home and cried all the way back."

"Girl, I know you were under a lot of stress," said Cynthia.

"It was a difficult time for my entire family as well, as for each of you. I want to officially thank each of you for your love and support during this period in our life. All of you acted as my extended family, to which I will forever be in your debt. So today, lunch is on me."

"You don't have to do that Ann, we just want to get with you and welcome you back," said everyone.

"I know. However, I really want to say thank you for your support as great co-workers and as great friends."

"Okay, you have twisted ours arms," all of them said.

Cynthia brought up the fact that Douglas was the real person to be honored.

"You know he never complained about helping out one bit. He was willing to do anything we asked him to do."

"You are right about that, Cynthia. I have thanked him many times. I wish he were here with us so he could hear you say that. I will always be in his debt."

"I don't know if I would say it like that Ann, said Sheila.

"Douglas may have had someone in his car today, but I know by the way he mopes around the building that he still has the hots for you."

"No you are wrong about that Sheila. Douglas and I have gotten over that phase in our friendship. We talked about a lot of things while I was out. My dedication to Robert is stronger because of the conversations I have had with Douglas."

"Yes," said Flora. He kind of makes you see yourself in a different light doesn't he."

"Well, that is Mr. Douglas Brown. Always making you see something positive on the other side of the rainbow."

"That is so true Ann, but he is lucky," said Flora.

"What do you mean?" I asked Flora.

"Well, if he had given me opportunity months ago. I would have shown him my pot of gold on this side of the rainbow."

The entire group started to laugh. We finished off our salads and I answered minor questions concerning my leave. It was a very positive lunch. We all rode back to the office and didn't mention Douglas' name once. I know all of them sensed that I had grown closer to Douglas, but I did not let them know how close.

~ Chapter Twenty-Seven ~

Second Time

"Good night everyone," I said as I was leaving the building. My first day back at work wasn't what I wanted it to be when I left home this morning. However, I have a better perspective on what I should or should not wish for. Douglas was lucky that he was not at work today. But I may have been luckier. At least today helped me deal with the fact that I have some sort of feelings for Douglas. I know it is wrong. It is hard to understand why a physical attraction sometimes occurs so strongly between two people. For my sake, I hope I can put this desire behind me. I don't want to throw away all I have worked so hard for in my relationship with Robert. Suddenly my phone rang.

"Hello."

"Hey, Ann, are you on your way home?"

"Yes, Robert, I will pull in the driveway in a minute or two."

"That is great. I have been waiting all day with anticipation for you to come home."

"Why is that Robert?"

"I think it is because you were a little scared this morning and felt that you had to hold back because of my heart attack."

"I know, Robert, I am sorry."

"I know you thought I didn't remember but I do, Ann."

"I am parking Robert. I will be in the house in a minute."

I hung up the phone. I opened the door and there stood Robert dressed in nothing but his birthday suite and a vase of flowers.

"I am so sorry my love. It all came back to me today. I was taking a bath and I suddenly remembered you left to take a shower after we made love. It popped in my head. It was clear. We had just returned from your opening day ceremony at your new collection department. I was drinking some wine when you left to take a shower. I felt a little faint and that was the last thing I remembered until I saw you in the ICU room."

"Robert, I was so scared. I didn't know what to do. My only thoughts were that I almost killed you. I could not forgive myself."

"I know, Ann, but it wasn't your fault. It was mine. I had been working entirely too hard. Plus, I should have been careful about working long hours. I also believe that the good Lord has given me an angel to watch over me."

"Oh, Robert, I am so sorry. I am glad you can remember. Maybe now I will not be afraid of making love to you. I have been scared that you will have a heart attack."

"There is no need to worry. I will be fine, Ann. Go and freshen up. When you finish taking a shower I will be here waiting on you."

"Okay, Robert."

I gave a Robert a soft kiss and started to take my clothes off piece-by-piece leaving a line all the way to the bedroom. I could see Roberts's getting excited. I turned my back to him slowly walking away. I stopped and removed the rest of my clothing. As I looked back, Robert started to follow me. I threw my stockings at him. Somehow he managed to catch them with his teeth. I turned on the shower and jumped inside. I took a few minutes to make sure I was ready for whatever came next.

As I exited the shower, Robert appeared with a towel to wipe the water off my body. He started at the back of my neck. As he wiped each area, he gave me a soft kiss to confirm he did not leave a drop of water. Down my back he wiped with the towel. I could feel the towel moving down the slope of my body. Robert paused briefly to kiss me. He then continued to wipe the water from my legs. We moved to the bedroom where I sat on the edge of the bed as he dried my feet. He picked up the bottle of lotion from the night stand and rolled me onto my stomach. Hours passed as he gave me a complete massage. I felt totally relaxed.

"So what do you think of that, Ann?"

"I think you are back in proper form. I really needed that."

"I really needed you Ann. My confidence has been restored. I am ready to go back to work and get in the saddle again."

"I believe you may be ready to do just that Robert. But first, let us get cleaned up and take a shower together."

"Okay, Ann, I know you don't want to leave me alone. I feel good and strong.

"I see, Robert, but we don't want to over do it."

Robert and I took a shower together. I wasn't about to leave him alone for a second. I couldn't bare the thought of him having another heart attack. I was happy that Robert was okay. I needed to feel safe in his arms again.

~ Chapter Twenty-Eight ~

A Little Piece of Happiness

"It wasn't a dream," I said to myself.

She was lying next to me. The light in the room accented her beauty. Her lips looked moist and full. The night sleep and our heated exchanged of passion had not disturbed the sweetness that was held captured within her. I took in a deep breath as I lay there looking up at the ceiling. I felt my love for her flowing deep within me. I tried to draw a comparison of my love for her and my love for previous ladies that I had known. I could not think of one feeling that I had for another. At that very moment, she had no equal. It was as though I was given a gift. Yes, I was given a little piece of happiness to have as my own. I knew I could not have her. But, I could savor the experience and enjoy the feelings of love that I had for her. Right here and right now, I was as content as I had ever been in my life. If I had died at that exact moment, I would have been happy. My life would have stood for something and my love would have made a difference. In some odd way, I felt that angels were looking down at me smiling.

I laid there looking at her for an hour. I went over every kiss and every look we shared during the night. I thought about each sound she made. I felt each movement of her body as if we were making love. I felt the touch of her hands sliding down my shoulders. Her tongue played with my lips beckoning me to let it in. I felt her body move closer to mine pressing ever so softly against my skin. Her arms were my bed pillow, as I lay there consumed in the moment. Her chest pressed up against mine. I felt as if I was on a wave on the ocean. We moved together remaining in perfect rhythm. We stayed together until our love flowed over the satin sheets we laid upon. It was a powerful experience. We were caught in a moment in time where love and happiness were married. They gave us the wisdom of love and the knowledge that self-happiness keeps relationships in perfect harmony.

As I opened my eyes she said,

"I love you Douglas."

"I have been looking at your face wondering what you were thinking."

"I have been thinking of how much I love you and how making love to you has changed my life. It has been a long time since I have seen you. I cannot believe I am back in Georgia with you. After the weekend we spent in Miami, I dreamed of this moment over and over in my mind. You were so gentle with me. You understood what I needed. Now that I am free to date again, I want to be the woman you could spend the rest of your life with."

It was not, Ann lying next to me. It was Stephanie. Did she hear me? What did I say? What do I say? It wasn't a dream. Ann was not here with me. How do I comment on the statement Stephanie made?

~ Chapter Twenty-Nine ~

The Friendship

The next day I arrived at work early. I wanted to talk to Douglas before the other staff arrived. He usually arrived fifteen minutes before anyone else did. I was fine now, but I felt I had unfinished business with him. Robert had extinguished the fire I had; however, there was still something within me I felt I needed to say.

As I continued to walk down the hallway, I could see a light coming from Douglas' office. It surprised me because his car was not in the front parking lot. My heart began to beat fast with every step I took. What was I going to say or do when I came face to face with him? I didn't know if I would jump in his arms or just stand there with my big mouth wide open not knowing what to say.

As I got closer to Douglas' office, I began to hear sounds as if he was having a conversation with someone. As I arrived at his door, I saw him setting on the corner of his desk talking with the lady I had seen him with leaving the restaurant. I knocked on the door and Douglas turned around surprised.

"Hello, Ann! You are back! I am so happy to see you. How is Robert?"

Douglas rattled off a hundred questions before I could ask about the lady that was sitting in his chair. He gave me a big hug and a kiss on the side of my face. I just stood there wondering about the identity of the lady at his computer.

"Ann, you remember Stephanie?"

"Actually I have tried to forget her." I said in a low voice that neither of them could hear.

"Hello, Stephanie."

"Hello, Ann. It is nice to see you again."

I felt like darkness had descended on the face of the earth. Here I stood wanting to discuss my dilemma with Douglas and who turns up to spoil my opportunity. Yes, there was Ms. Thang. Ms. Number two had returned. I guess the next words out of her mouth will be, "Are you still the number three girl around here?" I recall a similar situation three years ago. I stood in this exact spot when he introduced me to Stephanie for the first time."

"Are you alright, Ann?"

"Yes I am. I don't want to bother you, Douglas."

"There is no bother at all, Ann. What do you need?"

"Is it possible for you to come to my office for a minute or two?"

"Yes, Ann. I can tear myself away for a minute."

"Tear him self away!" "What in the world does he mean by that?" I asked myself. This encounter is becoming more disturbing by the second. I need to get this, "what ever I am feeling" out of me and Ms. Thang appears out of darkness to screw the moment up.

"Okay, Ann, I am here. What do you want to talk about?"

"Well, Douglas, I wanted to tell you in person how much I appreciate you helping me out when I was working from home. I hoped the kiss I gave you emphasized how much I really appreciated your help."

"It did, Ann. You don't know how much I had to fight the demons that were telling me to take advantage of that kiss. I really wanted to make love to you right then and there. It was just that the timing was not right. I couldn't do it in your house. I would not have been at my best and I would have been uncomfortable. However, if you were at my place I believe the demons would have been successful in convincing me to make love to you.

"I really appreciate your honesty, Douglas. I have felt the same way about the situation. I know that I am married to Robert but every now and then, life throws you a high fast ball right down the middle of the plate and you have to swing at it."

"Ann, I didn't know you understood baseball."

"Well, Douglas, I did work in Parks and Recreation center for several years. Plus, I have several cousins I grew up with who played sports. However, the point I am trying to make is that I began to have certain feelings for you and I needed to express them."

"I understand, Ann," said Douglas. But now that you are back with your number one lady I don't need to say anything but thanks for all you did for Robert and me."

"You know you are welcome, Ann. For you, I would do what it takes to put happiness in your life." We have traveled two diverse roads in life but we have found each other and become great friends."

"Thanks, Douglas! I know I still need to work these feelings out; however, I will somehow turn them into a positive way of looking at life."

"Ann, I will always be your friend. I will always be there no matter what road I must travel. There is something about you that holds my heart captive. I jump at every opportunity to put a little happiness in your life. I too have accepted that you are Robert's wife. But, if the two of you break up before I get married in the future. I hope you allow me to be the first to put my name in the hat."

"Thanks, Douglas. You are the best friend a woman could wish for. These last two months have made me wish I knew you had feelings for me before I met Robert. I think we would have made a great couple."

Douglas stood up and pulled me close to his chest and looked deep into my eyes and said, "With you, I have found my little piece of happiness and I will keep it with me for the rest of my life."

He kissed me on the lips and returned to his office. I knew we would always be friends. I had to suppress the feelings I have for Douglas and honor his friendship as he has honored mine all these years. It wasn't easy seeing him walk out my office knowing I would only be his good friend.

I retuned to my desk and smiled at the thought that I was willing to be a little more than a friend with Douglas. I opened up my desk draw and there was an envelope with my name on it. I opened it up and read the outside inscription.

"To Ann the best friend a man could have."

I took out the card that read:

"How can I put into words the feelings that live within my heart?

How can I describe the moment love first told me to look into your direction?

Is there a way to say I love you, so the words will have the power of the universe?

If I said I care for you, would you know each word means I love you deeply?

How can I show you the love inside of me?

What would be the measurement of truth?

If I held out my hand and asked you to look at my fading lifeline,

Would you know I had already given my life to you?

If Cupid stood before us and proclaimed my love for you was true,

Could you comprehend how great my love is?

If I told you that without your love I could not live,

would you give me all the love you could give?

Look into my eyes and you will see the words written in my heart.

They are but a few.

There is no other way to say "I love you."

Signed Douglas,

"Thanks for my little piece of happiness"

Printed in the United States
72523LV00007B/7